Old-Time Camp Meeting . . .

"Freeze it right there, slope."

Remo and Chiun turned toward the source of the unfamiliar voice. When a man clad in black stepped into the clearing, Karen screamed. "It's them," she squeaked. Her hands shook violently.

The soldier was big, nearly Remo's size, with powerful shoulders and a broad, craggy face. The Uzi submachine gun he was holding was pointed directly at Chiun.

Out of the corner of his eye, Remo saw seven more men fan out around the campsite. They were dressed in black as well, each one carrying a snub-nosed Uzi. They moved well, as if accustomed to the mechanics of ambush. Silently they formed a wide circle around the civilians, sealing off all exits.

"The girl. Hand her over. Otherwise the old gook gets it between the eyes."

"She is not yours to take," Chiun said.

"Oh, no?" The team leader's eyes shone with amused malice in the moonlight. "Just watch me."

He began to squeeze the trigger. . . .

THE DESTROYER series from Pinnacle Books:

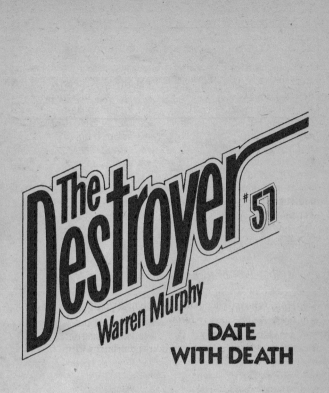

The Destroyer #57

Warren Murphy

DATE WITH DEATH

PINNACLE BOOKS   NEW YORK

DESTROYER #57: DATE WITH DEATH

An original Pinnacle Books edition, published for the first time anywhere.

First printing/October 1984

ISBN: 0-523-41567-2

Can. ISBN: 0-523-43102-3

Cover art by Hector Garrido

Printed in the United States of America

PINNACLE BOOKS, INC.
1430 Broadway
New York, New York 10018

9 8 7 6 5 4 3 2 1

CHAPTER ONE

The shack was made out of bits and pieces. Cardboard mostly, plus the remains of several packing crates and a couple of dented tin signs stolen from a nearby construction site. The floor was hard-packed earth covered with a patchwork of fraying straw mats. There were no windows. Just an opening that served as a door, and a fist-sized hole in the roof to ventilate the smoke from the kerosene lamp.

Inside the tiny shack, seven people were sitting cross-legged around a makeshift table. Six of them were members of the Madera family. The seventh, the one nearest the door, was their honored guest. The guest's name was Wally Donner, and at the moment he wasn't feeling well. In fact, if he didn't get some fresh air soon, he was going to be sick, violently, eruptively sick, and that didn't fit into his plans at all.

Donner's face glistened under a sheen of sweat, and his

sopping stay-press shirt was permanently glued to his back and shoulders. Along with the heat, his legs were starting to cramp up from sitting so long on the floor. But the worst of it was the smell, the almost indescribable odor of six unwashed bodies packed into a space not much bigger than his walk-in closet back home.

Donner took a deep breath, forcing himself to ignore his surroundings. He had to concentrate on the job, the only thing that really mattered. He was here to sell a dream, a vision of a distant, glittering place. It wasn't nearly so easy as he'd first thought it would be. Sometimes you had to make people imagine that place, to see it clearly in their minds. And like all good dream merchants, Donner tried to remember the first and only rule of the game: *Keep your mind on the dream.*

"Everyone get enough to eat?" he asked with a big, friendly grin. His voice was deep and soothing. In the sputtering lamp light his damp blond hair looked like burnished gold. His pale blue eyes were bright with feverish excitement.

"It was truly a feast," Consuela Madera murmured politely. She was the oldest of three sisters, and the best-looking. Donner had met her just a few minutes after he'd parked the van under a dusty piñon tree in the village square. From the moment he saw her, he knew she was exactly what his employer was looking for. The two younger Madera girls were acceptable, too. Both ebony-haired beauties in their own right, they had turned out to be an unexpected but welcome bonus.

"It's nothing," Donner said, gesturing expansively over

the litter of torn Cheese Doodles wrappers and bags that had once contained Ring Dings and Devil Dogs. "In America, this would be no more than a snack." Just looking at the chocolate-smeared cellophane made Donner's stomach turn, but he kept smiling.

"Such things are easily bought in America?" Miguel Madera asked hopefully. He was the family's only son, a fat, wheezing lump with dull, lusterless brown eyes and near-terminal cases of bad breath and acne. He'd eaten almost as much as the rest of the family put together. For a while, Donner thought he was going to have to go back to the van for another armload of goodies.

"You can get them just about anywhere north of the border," Donner assured them. "And with the kind of money we're offering, you could fill whole rooms with the stuff."

The announcement set off a burst of excited chatter among the Maderas. They lapsed into the local dialect, a weird blend of Spanish and some guttural-sounding Indian language. Donner spoke fluent Spanish, but he could only understand every fourth or fifth word of what they were saying. It irritated him.

He felt a faint breeze and turned his head quickly toward the flow of fresh air. His stomach settled down a little, but the stench remained. It was the thick, clinging smell of poverty, as unmistakable in its own way as the scent of $50-an-ounce perfume.

"Tell us again about the dwelling places," Consuela requested with a smile.

"Each of you will have a room of your own," he

3

explained. "A room ten times the size of this place. There will be thick carpets, wall to wall, air conditioning, and hot water. And of course, as I promised, a color television in each and every room."

"It all sounds so fantastic," Consuela murmured. She tilted her head in contemplation. The dim, wavering light emphasized the bold curve of her high cheekbones and the coppery glow of her skin. Her black hair shimmered with gold highlights.

She was a beauty, all right, Donner thought. No matter that in twenty years she'd look like every other potato-bodied broad in Mexico. For now, she was just right. She would serve his purpose well.

"What exactly would we have to do in return for all this?" she asked.

He flashed his most charming smile. "Why, whatever you'd like," he crooned. "Arrange flowers, decorate, shop. Anything that's fun." He gave her hand a pat.

Consuela nodded, not trusting herself to speak. She knew such things were possible, even true. She'd crossed the border herself last year, wading across the muddy Rio Grande by night with a dozen others, carrying a few things wrapped in cloth on her head. The border patrol had been waiting for them on the American side. When the aliens were spotted, men in trucks chased them, cutting great holes in the darkness with their glaring searchlights. But Consuela had managed to evade them long enough to spend three whole days with her cousin, who worked as a housekeeper in El Paso. The border patrol caught up with her there. After a night in a detention center, they'd sent her back home on a bus. But she'd seen the wonders by then and knew them to be true.

"A few months ago," she said slowly, "another man offered to take us across the border. But he wanted us to pay him a hundred dollars apiece, in advance, and to hide in the trunk of his car, all of us together." She still shuddered at the memory of the grinning entrepreneur, with his pockmarked face and single gold tooth that gleamed like an evil eye.

Donner laughed. "A coyote."

"Pardon?"

"A coyote," Donner said. "A professional smuggler of aliens. Well, I'm not one of them. I don't want any money from you people. My employer is covering all the expenses. We'll be crossing the border in style." He gestured toward the shiny new Econoline parked outside the door. "No hiding in trunks with me."

"But the border guards—"

"Arrangements have been made with the authorities for you to cross over without any of the usual bother."

It all sounded so impossibly wonderful to Consuela, and yet she found herself hesitating over the offer. She didn't have the slightest idea why. "What about the *carta verde*?" she asked. "My cousin said that you must have one to be able to work in America."

"No problem," Donner replied. He smiled to cover his growing irritation while he reached into the pocket of his wilted shirt and slipped out a slender stack of "green cards," the necessary document for aliens working stateside. "We'll fill them in later," he said, fanning them out like a

5

conjurer about to perform a trick. When everyone had gotten a good look at them, he tucked them safely away again.

"Well?" he prompted Consuela. He knew she was the one to convince. If she went for it, the others would follow along.

"But *why*?" she asked. Her forehead wrinkled in confusion. "Why us? We have done nothing special to merit this good fortune."

Donner leaned forward conspiratorially. "Well, I'm not supposed to tell, but . . ." He let his words trail off into enigmatic silence. The Maderas leaned toward him in anticipation.

"We don't say nothing," Miguel said finally, asserting his authority over the family. "What you say, it don't go no farther than this room, okay?"

Donner made a point of staring at the Mexican for a moment, as if trying to decide. Then, once the tension was unbearable, he nodded. "All right," he sighed. "You're a tough negotiator, you know that?"

Miguel grinned proudly. The women looked at their brother with adoration.

"It began in the early days of television with an American show called 'The Millionaire,' " Donner said.

One of Consuela's sisters clapped her hands together. "Oh, yes! Our uncle's friend in America wrote to him about it before he died. A rich man gave away money to strangers."

"Is that what this is?" Consuela asked. "A gift from a millionaire?"

Donner shrugged. "I can say no more. Just bear in mind that there are many, many wealthy people in the United States."

"It is the land of opportunity," Miguel said stolidly. "In America, it is every man's right to be rich. Even if a man does not work, the government gives him a hundred times more money than we make here, just so he can be rich. It is called welfare."

"You'll do even better than the folks on welfare do if you come with me," Donner said.

The family went into a huddle again, switching back to the local dialect. Donner's stomach pitched and heaved. He really was going to have to get some fresh air soon. The bullcrap he'd been handing out was piling up so thick and fast, he could barely see his way through it. "The Millionaire," for God's sake, he thought. These dodos would believe anything.

A hovering *jijene* landed on his arm. Donner crushed the sand fly with a slap and then flicked the miniature corpse away with a snap of his fingers. What in hell was taking them so long? As if to make the waiting less tolerable still, the family dog sauntered in, hoisted a leg, and decorated the wall with an aromatic yellow stream. Donner suppressed an almost overpowering urge to reach out and snap its scrawny neck.

He shifted his attention back to the family. Consuela and her mother were talking in a barely audible whisper. The old woman's face remained expressionless. She looked more Indian than Mexican, with angular features and hooded eyes that never stopped looking at Donner. It gave him an uneasy feeling. The old lady almost looked as if she knew what he was up to. Maybe there was something in the blood, he thought, something passed on from that long-ago time when the first *conquistador* slipped the short end of the stick to one of her ancestors.

Out of long habit, Donner slid his hand beneath the table just to make sure that the Ruger Blackhawk was still nestled comfortably in his ankle holster. He liked to play things safe, to always have an edge, even though he rarely had to use it. Donner gave his Rolex a meaningful tap. "It's getting late," he said good-naturedly. "I don't want to rush you, but . . ." He grinned and spread his arms. "If you're not interested, I'll have to get some other family. The rules, you understand."

"We're coming with you," Consuela said firmly. Her mother continued to eye Donner suspiciously, but the old man squeezed Donner's shoulder and exposed two yellowing teeth in a smile. The two younger daughters started giggling. Miguel's eyes brightened at the prospect of unlimited Ring Dings. Even the dog looked pleased.

"I applaud your good sense," Donner said. "You're really going to love it in America. I'll be waiting outside." He rose unsteadily to his feet. "Don't take too long packing. And no saying good-bye to the neighbors," he warned them. "They would only be envious of your good fortune and might tell the wrong people." With that final cautionary note, he groped his way out of the shack, gulping down air to quell his heaving stomach.

He leaned against the van, smoking a cigarette while he kept a watchful eye on the Maderas' shack. Three in one, he congratulated himself. Consuela was perfect, just what his employer demanded. The face of a queen, and the body of a harlot. It was a damn shame she was Mexican.

For as long as he could remember, Donner had hated all things even remotely Mexican. Just looking at a bag of Doritos nauseated him. He cringed every time he drove by a Taco John's. Mexicans were, as far as he was concerned, the scum of the earth. This negative national bias was particularly unpleasant for Wally Donner because he was, in fact, half-Mexican himself. Even his real name was half-Mexican. José Donner. He hated it.

He had no real memory of his father, a gaunt, smiling blond man who disappeared one night a few months after Donner's birth. For years the man's silver-framed portrait sat on top of the TV. José's mother began each morning by dusting the portrait, after which she started on her ironing—shirt after shirt after shirt, all belonging to the wealthy men who lived up on the hill. While she ironed, Donner's mother spoke to her infant son in a constant flow of softly accented Spanish. She told him stories and legends, bits of folklore and gossip, anything to relieve the tedious repetition of her work.

Young Donner never played with the neighborhood kids. Few visitors came to the family's peeling stucco bungalow. It was rarer still that mother and son ventured outside. As a result, Donner was a full five years old before he found out that English wasn't just a language spoken on TV. He learned the lesson the hard way—on his very first day at school. He looked so American, with his blond hair, blue eyes, and rosy complexion, but all that came out of his mouth was "beaner" talk.

The white kids hated him. The Mexican kids hated him. The handful of blacks and Chinese just thought he was too funny for words. Young Donner spent the whole day fighting one kid after another. At the end of the day, he dragged himself home determined to learn American even if it meant that he never spoke to his mother again.

His teacher was the television set. In a way, it became his home, too. Every evening he escaped into the ordered, happy world of "The Donna Reed Show," "Father Knows Best," and a dozen other similar shows. People had *whole* families on TV. They lived on pretty, tree-lined streets and washed their hands before dinner. The mother, regardless of the show, always wore earrings and high heels. Best of all, nothing really bad ever happened on TV sitcoms. Sure, the characters had their problems, but no matter how dire they were, everything seemed to turn out all right before the last commercial.

Donner's favorite was "Leave It to Beaver." No one on earth was more wholesomely American than Wally Cleaver. Wally was a charmed soul. Donner could remember thinking that Wally Cleaver could have beaten an old lady over the head with an ice axe, and everything would still have been all right as long as he shuffled over to his father, hands in pockets and looking toothy and cute, and said, "Gee, Dad."

So Donner watched, and learned. The years passed quickly, undistinguished by their sameness. Young Donner continued to fight by day and watch television by night, tuning out his mother's incessant babbling as he concentrated on the tiny flickering screen. It didn't take him long to learn American. He knew even then that the language had always been inside him. It was just a matter of getting his tongue to shape the words. He tried desperately to forget Spanish at the same time, but he just couldn't force it out of his mind. He finally had to admit defeat. It was with him for life, like some hideous birthmark that only he could see in the mirror.

At fifteen he left home, slipping quietly away one Sunday morning while his mother was at church. It wasn't anything he'd planned. He just woke up that morning knowing that it was time to go. He packed a few things in his gym bag and headed up the street, not bothering to close the door behind him. He didn't bother with a note, either. His mother would know he was gone for good when she saw the shattered picture frame on the TV and the smiling blond man's face torn and distorted under the shards of broken glass. And if she was dumb enough to think that was an accident, she only had to check the old Whitman's candy box where she kept the household money. Once she looked inside it, she'd know the truth for sure.

That very first night on his own, Donner got a lift from a lady in a Cadillac Eldorado. He remembered her even now, that bright and brittle blond hair, the folds of tanned, wrinkled skin around her neck, the way her carmine-tipped fingers drummed a nervous tattoo on the steering wheel.

She asked him what his name was. His lips started to form the sound, "José," but what came out instead was "Wally."

"Wally. That's cute."

"Gee, Ma'am, thanks," Donner had said.

It was the beginning.

She told him she felt sorry for him, a big, healthy-looking boy like himself all alone in the world like that. Her sympathy took the form of an invitation. She thought it might be nice if Donner stayed with her for a few days.

The few days turned into a month, and Donner spent it learning some new and interesting things about his body, things he'd only just suspected before. In retrospect, he figured the old hag had gotten more than her money's worth. The three grand that Donner fled with worked out to a hundred a day. He knew he was worth that and a whole lot more besides.

He kept moving from town to town. He found there was always someone willing to help him out, to put a little folding green in his jeans for the right kind of services rendered. Still, there were those rare times when the pickings got lean. So, like any good businessman, Donner branched out into another line of work. Armed robbery was what they called it in most places.

He killed for the first time in Jackson Hole, Wyoming, when a liquor store clerk made the fatal mistake of going for the sawed-off under the counter. The memory was still vivid, like some cherished instant replay. The thunderous sound of the gun, the funny pattern the blood made as it spread across the clerk's faded plaid shirt, and the look of surprise on his face before he pitched over backward into a display of discount wines.

"We're ready," Consuela called out, interrupting Donner's thoughts. He forced a smile. "Then what are we waiting for?" He tossed away his cigarette and slid open the Econoline's passenger door. The interior looked comfortable and inviting, with shag carpet on the floor and plush-covered captain's chairs instead of the usual seats. All the side and rear windows had amber-tinted glass. If any of the Maderas thought that was a little odd, no one mentioned it.

"Let's go," Donner said, beckoning them. "It's a long way to the border."

With one fleeting backward glance at the shack, Consuela led her family across the litter-strewn yard. They carried their few possessions in cloth-wrapped bundles. Miguel had made an unsuccessful attempt to hide the family dog in the voluminous folds of his shirt, but the animal's slat-ribbed body kept squirming while its pink tongue lapped playfully at the Mexican's pudgy face. Donner decided to let it go. Why make a fuss now, when he could just as easily take care of it after they cleared the border? The Maderas filed into the van in respectful silence. When everyone was seated, Donner slid the door shut and turned the key in the lock.

He concentrated on his driving as he eased the van down the narrow, winding mountain road. There weren't many street lights or signs in this part of Chihuahua. Some of the out-of-the-way villages he'd been in didn't have so much as a single paved road. It was amazing how out of touch these people were, he thought, as if the twentieth century had passed them by without even bothering to wave. Still, it made his job easier. He'd tried the border towns when he'd first started. But they were too Americanized, too wary and hard-assed, too used to running their

13

own cons with little time left over to listen to his. Donner quickly realized that if you wanted to peddle a dream, you had to go where people still believed in them.

When he finally nosed the van onto the highway, Donner pulled out a bottle of tequila from beneath the seat. Behind him the Maderas were singing like a bunch of kids on a camping trip. They sang songs about love, revolution, death, and the Blessed Virgin. The constant rise and fall of their voices was beginning to grate on his nerves.

"Here's something to shorten the road a bit," he said, passing a straw-wrapped bottle back to the old man. Donner grinned as he heard the cork pop. "Let's drink a toast," he suggested, "to a new and better life in America."

"I'm sorry," Consuela said apologetically, "but spirits disagree with me. And my sisters are not yet old enough for such things."

"But you must," Donner insisted. "Surely your stomach is not as delicate as that. After all, this is a toast, an occasion of great honor and seriousness. Of course, if it means nothing to you . . ." He fell silent, as if he were suddenly overwhelmed by disappointment.

"All right," the girl conceded. "Just this once, in honor of the occasion."

Donner watched them pass the bottle in the rear-view mirror. It worked every time. All you had to do was appeal to a Mexican's sense of pride, and you could get him to do anything. By the time the tequila had gone full circle, the old man's head had slumped to his chest. The rest of the Maderas passed out a few seconds later. Donner heard the bottle hit the carpeted floor with a thud. The skinny yellow dog rose off his haunches and lapped up the last few drops before they soaked into the rug. A moment later he toppled over, too, his big brown eyes glazed and shining.

"Potent stuff," Donner chuckled. "Didn't anyone ever teach you shitheads not to drink with strangers?" Laughing, he goosed the van up to sixty. He was on the main highway now, only about an hour and a quarter shy of the border. Considering how much chloral hydrate he'd put in the tequila, it looked like the Maderas were going to miss their arrival in America.

Donner leaned back in his seat. It felt good to have the wind on his face and nothing but the clear, empty road up ahead. He teased a Winston out of the pack, lit up, and took a long, satisfying drag. His life had really changed a lot in the past few months. He could still remember how surprised he'd been when the first letter came. The way the thick wad of bills had spilled out of the envelope to form a ragged green pile across his threadbare living room rug. It was more money than he'd ever seen at one time, and the letter promised a great deal more.

The letter itself was short, simple, and businesslike. In return for all this sudden wealth, all he had to do was supply his anonymous employer with women. 242 women, to be exact. Specifications were given as to age and general physical attributes, but the type required would be very hard to find. Basically the guy wanted pretty women. That wasn't too difficult to understand.

There was only one catch to the deal. Donner couldn't

15

take women whose sudden disappearance would cause a big stir. In the letter his would-be employer suggested that he do most of his recruiting in Mexico, as they tended to be a bit more lax down there in the matter of missing persons. He informed Donner that arrangements had been made for him to cross and recross the border without the hassle of having his vehicle inspected. The final page of the letter gave detailed instructions on crossing points, times, even what lane to get in so that he could always be sure of connecting with a *simpático* border patrolman. Obviously, a great deal of money and time had already been spent on smoothing the way for this cross-border commute. Donner was even more impressed when he found the keys to a brand-new twelve-passenger van taped inside the envelope, along with a registration and a bill of sale, both in his name.

Donner had gone to the window and lifted the curtain slightly to peer outside. The van was parked right out front. He checked the license number against the registration. That was it, all right. What made these people so damned sure of themselves? Why had they picked him out of the thousands of people who lived in Santa Fe?

Another thought occurred to him. What was to prevent him from taking the money and the van and splitting for parts unknown? The thought gave him a warm feeling. Why not? Anyone trusting enough to give a stranger wheels deserved to be ripped off.

The whirlwind of ideas in his brain was interrupted by the shrill ringing of the telephone. Donner hesitated for a moment, annoyed, then lifted the receiver.

"You've read the letter?" the caller asked. The voice was clipped and cool, devoid of emotion.

"I read it," Donner said.

"Good. Now you have two choices," the caller continued smoothly. "One, you may enter my employ and partake of its numerous benefits. Or secondly, you may choose to turn down my generous terms. In that case, all you need do is place the envelope and its contents under the sun visor on the driver's side of the van. Someone will come by within the hour to drive the vehicle away. On the other hand, if you do accept my offer, I'll expect you to start work today."

"I really haven't thought . . ."

"Then think now," the cool voice said. "By the way, if you've been contemplating another alternative of your own devising, I suggest you put it out of your mind. The world is a big place, Mr. Donner, but not nearly big enough." With that final cautionary note, the line went dead.

Donner drew a deep breath and gently cradled the receiver. He was surprised to find that his hands were shaking. Any thoughts he'd had about disappearing with the van and money were gone. The man on the phone didn't sound like anyone to mess around with.

It only took a few minutes to decide. He would take the job. It was too damned good for him to pass up. The more Donner thought about it, the more he realized that this was just the kind of work he'd been cut out for from the very start. He had all the qualifications—the looks, the charm, and his fluent Spanish. And the fact that he killed without hesitation or remorse would help, too. Combine all of that

17

with the way he felt about Mexicans, and it added up to a perfect job for Wally Donner.

He experienced a momentary chill, as if an icy hand had gently reached out to caress him. It had just occurred to him that someone else must know virtually everything about him. And that someone else was the man he'd just decided to work for.

The chill passed. After a few days, Donner found himself caught up in his work, loving the sense of power it gave him, the way he could alter lives and destinies with a few nice words and a convincing smile.

Donner never gave much thought to what might happen to the women after he delivered them or to why his employer needed exactly 242. When it came right down to it, he really didn't care. He had his own future to think about. A future of wealth and respect, as far removed from the shabby wretchedness of his childhood as he could get.

Up ahead Donner could see the bright lights of Juárez. It was a border town like dozens of others, a little bigger than most, but still nothing more than bars, whorehouses, and shops filled with overpriced junk. The glaring pastel neon was an invitation to youthful tourists to lose their cherries and their wallets at the same time, with maybe a dose of clap thrown in as a souvenir of sunny Mexico.

He passed through the border checkpoint without incident. The grinning patrolman just went through the motions and then waved him through. Donner wondered as he often had before just how much those guys at the border were getting for their part in the operation. His anonymous employer really did know how to spread the green stuff around.

Stateside, Donner got caught up in the congested traffic of El Paso. Once he broke free, he sped on into New Mexico. He was in the home stretch now. Forty more miles to the rendezvous point and then back to the motel for a couple of cold ones and eight hours of well-deserved rest.

Donner was going so fast that he almost didn't see the hitchhiker. But a glimpse of wind-blown blond hair and long, tapering legs made him slam on the brakes. He poked his head out the window before backing up, just to make sure she was alone.

"Need a lift?" Donner smiled down at her.

"If you're headed toward Santa Fe, I do." The girl returned his smile. She looked to be eighteen, maybe twenty, with a pretty, dimple-chinned face framed by a tangle of honey-blond hair. She was wearing cutoffs that showed off her smooth, tanned legs and a plain white T-shirt that emphasized the size and shape of her breasts, especially where the fabric clung to them beneath the straps of her backpack.

"Climb aboard," Donner invited her. "I'm driving straight through to Santa Fe." As she circled around toward the passenger door, Donner took a quick look back at the unconscious Mexicans. The rear of the van was too dark to see anything more than indistinct shapes and shadows. Everything would be fine as long as the girl didn't get overly inquisitive about the back of the van.

"Thanks a lot," she said as the van picked up speed again. "I've been out there for hours."

"Guess you're a pretty lucky girl," Donner said. "What's your name?"

"Karen Lockwood," she said distractedly as the van turned onto a bumpy dirt road. "You . . . you're sure you're going to Santa Fe?"

"Absolutely," Donner assured her. "This is just a shortcut. It's the best way to avoid all the heavy traffic around Salinas."

The girl nodded tensely. She wanted to believe him, Donner realized. She was tired and lost, and she wanted to believe he was helping her. It worked every time. Give them a dream, and they'll keep on dreaming, even while you're sticking the knife in their ribs.

"This is pretty desolate country," he said casually. "I have to admit I'm a little surprised to find you out here all alone. Not that it's any of my business," he added quickly. "I guess I'm just a natural born worrier."

"Don't waste it on me," the girl said, grinning. Her right hand darted up, and a split second later it was wrapped around the bone handle of a wicked-looking bowie knife. She held it out in front of her, her arm rigid and rock-steady. The curving steel blade gleamed in the moonlight. "Don't get nervous," she told Donner. "I only use it as a means of self-preservation. I like to travel solo. Been all over the Southwest on my own." She slipped the bowie back into its sheath hidden away under her free-flowing curls.

"Ever have to use it?" Donner asked, his jaw clenching.

"Once or twice." She smiled. "Do you think we could stop for a minute once we get back on the interstate? At a gas station or a diner, anywhere I could pick up a Coke. My throat's starting to feel like an empty cactus.''

''The first place we see,'' Donner promised. He eased up on the gas and reached down under his seat. ''Try a shot of this,'' he offered, handing her a straw-wrapped bottle. It was just like the one the Maderas had passed around before the sudden urge to sleep came upon them.

''What is it?'' she asked warily.

''Santa Maria tequila. Alvaro grows wild around there, so the locals make their own home brew. It's strong stuff, but you look like you can handle it.''

''You'd better believe it,'' she said, grinning. She pulled the cork and took a long swallow. Less than a minute later, she was slumped against Donner's shoulder. He leaned over and eased the bottle out of her hand. No point in letting good liquor spill all over the place.

Up ahead, he noticed a deep arroyo about twenty yards from the road. Slowing down to twenty, he nosed the Econoline toward it. When he was as close as he could get, he cut the engine and climbed out. It was time for him to lighten his load, and this was as good a place as any. After all, he was only being paid to deliver women.

After removing the razor-edged bowie, Donner picked the girl up and tossed her in the back. ''Pleasant dreams, Karen Lockwood,'' he whispered. Then he dragged out Miguel, the old lady, and the old man. When the three of them were lying in the arroyo, out of sight now from anyone who might drive by, Donner unholstered the Blackhawk and screwed on a homemade silencer. ''Welcome to America,'' he said, smiling. Then slowly, carefully, he put a single shot through each of their heads.

Donner was too busy to notice the dog. It crawled out of the van and scrambled for the shelter of the rocks. There it stayed, quiet and still until the Econoline's taillights disappeared over the horizon. Only then did the dog come out to investigate. It circled the bodies twice, scratched at the ground, and then lifted its muzzle to howl balefully at the moon.

CHAPTER TWO

His name was Remo and he was sticking his finger into the barrel of a Smith & Wesson .38 and thinking they didn't make muggers like they used to.

It all started with Chiun's trunks. As usual, Remo's trainer had packed twenty-seven large lacquer boxes in preparation for a four-mile trip to the airport.

"We're only meeting Smitty for instructions," Remo protested. "If he weren't so paranoid, he'd call on the phone. We don't need all this luggage just to talk to him."

"Imbecile," the old Korean said. "Emperor Smith obviously wishes us to travel. An assassin sitting in a motel room is a useless thing."

"So is an assassin with twenty-seven steamer trunks," Remo said.

"Only if he is fettered by a slothful white pupil who spends his time arguing instead of attending to his duties."

"Funny. I thought my duty was to work for the guy who pays us."

"Only when necessary, O oatmeal-brained one. Your main duty is to tend to the needs of your frail and aging teacher in the twilight of his life. Now, get a taxi."

"*A* taxi?" Remo grumbled. "Try five. We'll need a caravan to get this stuff moved."

"The Master of Sinanju is not concerned with trivialities," Chiun said, picking an imaginary piece of lint off his green brocade robe. "Take care not to damage my Betamax."

"Which one?" Remo muttered, hoisting two of the trunks onto his shoulders.

"That one. It is the machine on which I view the history of your country."

Remo emitted a small whinny of defeat. What the old man considered a pictorial essay on America was, in fact, a soap opera named "As the Planet Revolves," which had been off the air for the past fifteen years. Chiun had his own sense of reality. People were disposable; characters on television were not. It was useless to argue.

Remo staggered out of the motel, set down the two trunks, and looked around for a taxi. There were none in sight. While he was looking, a small boy tossed a melting ice cream bar on one of them. A stray dog came over and licked it up, then lifted its leg on the trunks. On the near corner, a youth leaned against the lamp post, methodically picking his teeth with a stiletto while he eyed the gleaming brass clasps. It wasn't the part of town where you left your luggage on the street to hunt a cab.

The clock down the block read 10:49. He was supposed

24

to meet his employer, Smith, at exactly eleven o'clock. The way things were going, he'd be lucky to make it to the airport by sunset.

A ray of hope flickered dimly at the sight of the yellow-clad figure walking toward him. The boy's freshly shaven head glistened in the sunlight. His bare feet made a soft swooshing sound as he padded down the debris-strewn sidewalk. In one hand he carried a brightly colored can while the other clamored away on a pair of finger cymbals.

Okay, Remo thought. The kid's a fruitcake, but these cultist zanies don't steal trunks full of civilian clothes. He smiled as the youth approached.

"Hare Krishna," the young man said in a thin but enthusiastic voice. He held the can under Remo's nose. "I'm collecting for the church of Krishna and his followers. A donation of five or ten dollars would be appreciated."

"I'll do better than that," Remo said, pulling out a roll of hundred-dollar bills. The youth's eyes popped as Remo peeled one off the top. "Look," Remo said. "I've got to go back inside for more of these. If you'll watch the trunks for me and hail a cab when one comes by, the C-note's yours."

The youth straightened up, suddenly indignant. "You want me to *do* something for it?"

"It didn't really seem like a lot to ask," Remo waffled.

"My work is for Krishna," the youth said witheringly. "We shun the greed of the West. Our lives are spent in contemplation, not in selling our labor for cash."

"Okay. It was only an idea."

"A dependence on money and material gain leads to

25

corruption of the spirit. When the spirit is corrupt, evil takes root. Greed breeds crime. The disintegration of humanity is . . .''

''All right already. I'll find somebody else.''

The youth dug into the folds of his gown. ''Wait a minute. I want you to see something.'' He pulled out a shiny black automatic. ''Do you know what this is?''

''I can take a wild guess,'' Remo said.

''I have been forced to protect myself against the evildoers of the world with this weapon. It pains me to carry it, but there are those who would actually rob the donations I've collected.''

As he spoke, he fingered the gun lovingly. ''If it weren't for this, I'd be helpless,'' he said.

''You're breaking my heart.''

The young man's eyes never left the automatic. ''It's really a man-stopper, you know,'' he said dreamily. ''If I decided to use it, I could get anything I wanted with this baby. All I'd have to do would be . . .'' Slowly he turned the barrel of the gun to face Remo.

''That's it, huh?''

''You got it. Where's that roll of bills you were flashing?''

''In my pocket. And it's going to stay there, Gunga Din.''

That was the point at which Remo stuck his finger into the barrel.

Things happened fast after that. The Krishna squeezed the trigger, but by the time the bullet left the gun, Remo had twisted the barrel into a loop pointing skyward.

''How'd you do that?'' the Krishna gasped.

"Like this." Remo picked the young man up by his ankles and twirled him into the configuration of a pretzel.

"It's only money!" the boy yelled, trying to disentangle himself. "In the end, money isn't worth much."

"Neither are you," Remo said. With a little spin, he thrust his arms upward. The boy spun twenty feet into the air.

"Establishment brutality!" the Krishna squeaked. He seemed to hover a speck in the sky.

Remo stood silently on the ground below, his arms folded.

"Well? Aren't you going to catch me?"

"Nope," Remo said.

"Then what's going to happen?" the youth called.

"Ever drop an egg into an empty swimming pool?"

The Krishna screamed. He negotiated as he descended. His saffron robe was wound around a pair of skinny legs. "Okay," he said huskily, trying to keep his voice calm. "You win. Here's the deal. You catch me, and I walk away, all right?"

Remo considered. "I think I'd rather watch the old egg trick." Remo slapped him skyward again.

"The can. You can keep the can with all the donations in it."

"No thanks. Money is far too evil and corrupting. Death is much more satisfying. Especially yours."

The boy was sobbing. "What do you want, mister? I'll do anything." He was low enough now that passersby could see his red jockey shorts beneath his robe.

"Anything?" Remo asked.

"Anything. Please, mister. Just catch me."

A second before impact, Remo stuck out his toe, grazing the boy's back so that he turned in a gentle somersault that broke his fall. Then Remo caught him by the scruff of the neck.

"You said anything, right?"

"Yeah," the youth said sullenly.

"Yes, sir," Remo corrected. "Or I send you right back up."

"Yes, sir!" the boy shouted.

"Good," Remo said. "You've got potential."

"For what?"

"The army. You're going to join."

"The *army*? Are you crazy?"

Remo exerted the smallest pressure on the base of the boy's neck.

"I mean, yes, sir!"

A yellow taxi pulled up alongside them. "Now I get a cab," Remo sighed. He handed the driver a hundred-dollar bill. "Take this twerp to the Army Recruiting Center," he said.

"I got no change," the cabbie said.

"Call five of your buddies on duty to come here, and you can keep it." He shoved the boy into the back seat and slammed the door. "Uncle Sam needs you," he said in parting.

Like a kick in the pants, Remo thought after the cab pulled away. Well, what the hell. It was worth a try, and it was better than killing the kid. Even a professional assassin couldn't go around murdering every cretin who rubbed him the wrong way.

But what had made him think of the army, Remo wondered as he began the endless task of carting Chiun's trunks from the motel room to the waiting taxis. His own time spent in service had been so long ago. Long ago and better forgotten, along with the rest of the life that used to belong to him.

More than ten years since he'd left the army to become a cop.

More than ten years since he'd ceased to exist.

According to all his records, Remo Williams was a dead man. He had died in an electric chair for the crime of killing a dope pusher. It had been all smoke and no fire, though, a clever magician's illusion. In the end, Remo had not been fast-fried. This was a twisted bit of poetic justice, because he hadn't offed the pusher to begin with.

It was all part and parcel of an elaborate frame-up engineered by one Harold W. Smith. All the strings had been pulled from a comfortable chair that was parked in front of a computer console secreted away in the depths of Folcroft Sanitarium in Rye, New York. Like some mad prestidigitator, Smith had pulled off one macabre trick after another to make Remo into the nonperson he wanted. A fraudulent arrest, a fraudulent trial, and then a fraudulent death, cheated by Smith's sleight of hand. The performance had been planned down to the last detail, even to the substitution of another body for Remo's.

All this had taken place for the sole purpose of providing Harold Smith with a man who officially did not exist. Remo was a perfect candidate: an orphan without family ties, a rogue cop who was dead, buried, and soon to be lost to memory.

After Remo regained consciousness a few days after his bogus electrocution, he learned the bizarre destiny that he was expected to fulfill. Remo was to be the sole enforcer for CURE, an illegal organization developed by Harold W. Smith for the United States government. CURE's purpose was to fight crime outside the limits of the Constitution.

Smith's orders for CURE came directly from the President of the United States—the only other individual besides Smith and Remo who knew of the organization's existence. Even Chiun, Remo's trainer and teacher, had no real knowledge of how CURE worked. As far as Chiun was concerned, he was preparing Remo for the task of protecting Harold W. Smith after Smith had usurped the crown of the United States and proclaimed himself Emperor of America.

It was how the ancient Masters of the Korean village of Sinanju had earned their keep for thousands of years. Sinanju was a poor village, with nothing to trade for food. Its only asset was a physical power that in lesser hands, in later years, came to be known as martial arts. The Masters of the fighting techniques of Sinanju were the greatest killers on the face of the earth, and it was this ability they eventually rented to rulers of other lands in order to support their village.

Traditionally, each Master of Sinanju trained a pupil to take his place after he was gone. Untraditionally, the present Master of Sinanju—Chiun—had been saddled with a full-grown white man as his apprentice. That was part of Harold W. Smith's contract with Chiun. The old Oriental was to train Remo Williams in exchange for a submarine full of gold bullion to be delivered yearly to the village of Sinanju.

At first, Chiun had thought it would be an impossible task to teach a soft, meat-eating white the secrets of the most difficult discipline of all the martial arts. But with time, even the old Master had to admit that Remo possessed an almost uncanny aptitude.

Remo, for his part, resented having his identity snuffed out by a computer system, and resisted strongly Smith's mandate that he become a professional assassin. There was something vaguely un-American about the vocation Smith had chosen for him.

But Smith talked and Remo thought about the day an assassin's bullet snuffed out the life of the very president who had founded CURE. It was obvious that such evil could only be countered by an equally deadly force. Two minutes after his inauguration, the new president was offered and accepted the awesome burden of CURE's continued existence.

The memories faded as Remo walked back into the motel room for the thirteenth time.

"Let's go, Little Father," Remo puffed as he picked up the last three trunks.

Chiun waved him away distractedly. He was sitting on one of the beds in the room, engaged in rapt conversation with the chambermaid.

" 'All My Relatives' is pretty good," she said knowledgeably, "but there was nothing like 'As the Planet Revolves.' It was my all-time favorite." She stubbed out a cigarette in an ashtray overflowing with lipstick-tipped butts.

"Mine, too!" Chiun squealed. The white hair on his head and chin bobbed in agreement.

"That Rad Rex is a dreamboat." She shifted her pink nylon uniform around her massive thighs. "What a hunk."

"And Mona Madrigal," Chiun rhapsodized. "The loveliest of women. Perhaps she is Korean."

"Maybe so," the maid said, creasing her forehead with thought. "I mean, she was short and everything. It didn't say so in this magazine article I read. It just said she got divorced."

"What a pity," Chiun said, clucking in sympathy. "But then, only the most extraordinary of men could please one so beautiful as Mona Madrigal."

The maid shrugged. "I dunno. It said she was living in Santa Fe."

"Don't you have some work to do?" Remo asked irritably.

The maid snorted and lumbered to her feet. Chiun patted her hand. "Don't mind him," the old man whispered. "Some people have no soul."

"It's a side effect that comes from breaking your back," Remo groused as he shuffled out of the room with the trunks.

Harold Smith was heavily disguised. Instead of his usual three-piece gray suit, steel-rimmed glasses, and briefcase, he was wearing a brown three-piece suit, steel-rimmed glasses, and carrying a briefcase. It was as much imagination as he had ever shown.

"Don't act like you know me," Smith muttered as he

passed Remo and Chiun in the airport corridor. ''Meet me at Gate Twenty-seven.''

''As you wish, Emperor,'' Chiun said, bowing low. ''We will tell no one that we are to meet you at Gate Twenty-seven. Your loyal assassins are at your service at all times, O illustrious one. . . .''

''I think he wants us to ignore him, Little Father,'' Remo said.

''Nonsense. No emperor wishes to be ignored. It is why they desire to be emperors.''

''Smitty's not an emperor,'' Remo said flatly. He had explained Smith's status to Chiun almost daily for the past ten years.

''Of course not. Heh heh. One does not wish to be called emperor while the current emperor still holds the throne. Heh heh.''

''Forget it,'' Remo said.

Gate twenty-seven was crowded with passengers lining up for boarding. Smith pretended not to notice the dark-haired young man with the exceptionally thick wrists and the old Oriental dressed in flowing robes as they sat next to him in the waiting area.

''You're late,'' he said, his New England accent twanging acerbically.

''Best I could do,'' Remo said.

''Well, never mind that. There isn't much time. You're to board that plane.'' He nodded toward the line of passengers moving up the ramp.

''Where're we going?''

''New Mexico. There's been a rash of unexplained murders in the mesa.''

''So? They've got police in New Mexico.''

''A rash. More than three hundred in a matter of weeks. All unidentified. Mexicans, by their clothes and features. No similarities as to age, sex, occupation—only in the method of execution. They all died of single bullet wounds in the head.''

''What about the FBI?''

''They've been called in, but they've gotten nowhere. At first they suspected that the bodies belonged to Cuban spies, but they've given up on that. Then the CURE computers came up with a couple of interesting facts. One is that the murders seem to correlate to a dramatic increase in reports of missing persons coming out of Mexico.''

''You mean they were missing in Mexico, and dead in New Mexico?''

''They're not the same people. For the past few weeks, most of the people reported missing have been young women. None of the murder victims found in the desert have been young women. Not one. It's the only consistency in the pattern.''

''Doesn't sound like much of a lead. What's the other information?''

''It may not be anything, but there's been a sudden increase in air traffic in and around the Sangre de Cristo Mountains. That's in the same general area as the murders.''

''Air traffic? Are they shooting these guys from helicopters?''

''No. The wounds on the bodies were inflicted at close

range from a handgun. A Ruger Blackhawk. It's one killer who's doing all the damage, but he won't be easy to find. The mesa's a big area. And if this business goes on much longer, the press is bound to get hold of the story and terrify the whole Southwest. When that happens, the killer will almost certainly go into hiding, and we'll miss any chance of catching him. The president's concerned.''

Remo nodded. ''I thought my cop days were over,'' he said.

''Somebody has to do it,'' Smith said, rising. It was his favorite phrase, covering every unpleasant task Remo had to perform, from killing unlucky witnesses to swabbing up bodies.

''By the way, I've arranged to have a car for you at the airport in Santa Fe,'' Smith said. He slipped Remo a circular wire with two dirty keys dangling from it.

''Smitty, you're a prince.''

''An emperor,'' Chiun hissed.

''Save your flattery,'' Smith said. ''I knew you'd need a car, and this was the only way I could think of to keep you from stealing one. It's a blue 'fifty-five Chevrolet.''

He walked away. On his seat were two tickets. When Remo picked them up, Chiun snatched them out of his hands.

''I thought he said Santa Fe, but I could not believe my good fortune,'' the old man shrieked.

''Uh, yeah,'' Remo said uncertainly, taking the tickets back. ''Santa Fe's supposed to have some nice sunsets.''

''No, no. That is not why we are going to this place. It is where Mona Madrigal lives.''

"Oh," Remo said. Gently he nudged Chiun into the boarding line. "That's great. What a fantastic coincidence."

"This is no coincidence," Chiun said stubbornly. "Is the daily rising of the sun a matter of coincidence? Obviously, Emperor Smith, in his divine and radiant wisdom, has seen fit to reward an old man for his many years of service. He has arranged for me to meet the lady of my dreams."

"Little Father," Remo said softly. "I don't want to hurt your feelings, but I'll lay odds Smitty's never even heard of Mona McGonigle, or whoever she is."

"Madrigal," Chiun snapped. "Do not be duped into believing that all men are as shallow and ignorant as yourself." He elbowed his way through the crowd to sit in his assigned seat.

"Insult me all you want," Remo said, "but Smitty's not going to come through on this one. We're going to Santa Fe on assignment."

"A mere ruse. If you knew the ways of emperors as I do, you would realize that this dead body business is merely a ploy to bring us to the city where Mona Madrigal dwells."

"So you can meet her," Remo said.

"Now you understand."

CHAPTER THREE

After slowly savoring the last morsel of chocolate torte, Miles Quantril put his fork down and patted his lips with a starched white linen napkin. "You may clear now," he murmured. He daubed his mouth one last time for good measure and then dropped the napkin on the china dessert plate.

An elderly, white-haired servant materialized at Quantril's side. Quickly and silently he cleared away the luncheon dishes, taking great pains not to spill a single crumb on Mr. Quantril's Savile Row suit. The butler had once made that mistake, and by way of reprimand, Quantril had kicked the servant in the buttocks. On particularly cold nights, the butler's hindquarters still throbbed dully even though the incident had taken place more than a year ago.

In his long career as a butler, the elderly gentleman's gentleman had worked for viscounts, barons, lords, and kings. None of them had ever put a boot up his butt for any reason. But then, none of them had ever paid half as well as Mr. Quantril. Now that he was nearing the age of retirement, the butler decided that money was a great deal more important than dignity. You couldn't bank a lifetime of good manners and refinement. So he would remain at his post until the end, and he would be especially careful not to spill the crumbs.

When the servant slipped silently out of the room, Quantril picked up the magazine beside him. It was open. From its pages, Quantril could see his own picture. He enjoyed reading about himself.

At thirty-three, he was tall and handsome and faultlessly groomed, from his razor-cut hair right down to his carefully manicured nails. Today he was dressed in one of his 280 custom-made suits, along with a color-coordinated shirt, tie, and pocket handkerchief. His black Italian loafers had been shined to mirrorlike perfection.

Miles Quantril lived up to the image of him projected from the pages of *Time* and *Newsweek* and *People*. Born of Old Money aristocracy, he was one of the richest and best-looking bachelors in the country. He was surrounded by wealth, pursued by beautiful women, and driven by work. "America's Favorite Tycoon," the magazine in his hand proclaimed. "Where Does He Go Next?"

"Where indeed?" Quantril whispered, his gaze passing over his penthouse office. The afternoon sunlight flooded the glass-and-chrome desk resting atop the plush carpeting. A bank of computers lined one entire wall. Another wall was covered with the rich leather bindings of a half-million-dollar collection of rare books. The office reflected just the right balance of power and elegance.

He smiled. "Oh, you have no idea, my friends, where I'm going to go next. No idea whatever."

Looking back, he realized that his success had been inevitable, with or without his family's fortune. He was a born leader.

He'd first felt the flush of power when he was six years old and caught the upstairs maid and the chauffeur screwing in the linen closet of his parents' mansion in Southampton. He blackmailed both servants for a hundred dollars apiece.

At prep school, Quantril became the youngest drug dealer in the history of the academy, a fact uncovered when he got caught by the school authorities. Were it not for a sudden large donation to the school's building fund from the Quantril family, young Miles might have been expelled. As it was, he was subjected to the severest punishment he had ever experienced: He was grounded for three months.

It was a sad time for Miles Quantril. He was twelve years old, with nothing to do but ride the thoroughbreds in the family stable, watch one of his three TV sets, swim in the Olympic-sized pool with its automatic wave machine, play in the private bowling alley in the basement, shoot grouse, and while away his spare time in the multimillion-dollar chemistry lab his father had given him for Christmas the year before. It was a wretched existence.

But Quantril persevered. In his lab, he discovered how to make bombs. They were crude at first, only blobs of plastique with varying amounts of nitroglycerine and TNT, but they improved with practice. Within six weeks, he was setting off land mines in the family rose garden. By the age of seventeen, he had developed an explosive powerful enough and accurate enough to blow up the local police headquarters.

He was arrested, but since the incident occurred three days before his eighteenth birthday, he was charged as a juvenile. His sentence was suspended by a judge who was a golfing partner of Miles's father.

"I'll take care of the boy in my own way," the elder Quantril promised.

And he did. Young Miles Quantril, one of the richest heirs in America, was cut off without a cent.

"I'll send you to college," his father said. "I'll give you an education. But that's all. No more allowance, no more cars, no more vacations on the Riviera. You're on your own."

Miles Quantril accepted the tuition money and went to college. Unfortunately, on the very day he left for the university, the generations-old Quantril mansion perished in an explosion of flame. Neither of his parents survived.

In college, he picked out the smartest kid in his dormitory, Bill Peterson, and asked him to write all his term papers for him.

"Why should I do that?" Peterson asked.

"No reason," Quantril said.

"Go screw yourself."

The next night, Bill Peterson's bed mysteriously caught fire.

When Peterson was released from the hospital, he volunteered to write all of Miles Quantril's papers for him.

From that beginning, it took little to organize all the straight-A students on campus into a term paper factory catering to the college's all-star football team.

The football players didn't pay Quantril for his service. Instead, they agreed to supply him with girls—the most curvaceous, beautiful, sexy girls in the state.

For a while, Miles Quantril was satisfied with having a different girl every night just for himself. But girls didn't make a man rich. One afternoon, as he was lying on his satin-sheeted bed while a gorgeous blonde panted between his legs, an idea occurred to him. The idea was brilliantly simple. It smacked of riches to come.

Its name was Dream Date.

Dream Date, as Quantril visualized it, would be a dating service. But unlike other wholesale matchmakers that saddled their customers with partners as unattractive and dull as they themselves were, Dream Date's clients would get only the best.

As proof, Quantril's customers would, for stiff fees, receive video cassettes of their intended partners, but the videos would be unlike anything else on the market.

Instead of seeing their potential mates as they really were, the recipients of Dream Date video cassettes would watch their fantasies come to life. Whatever they wanted—a Parisian aristocrat talking to them from the banks of the Seine, a harem beauty gyrating in transparent houri pants, a Chinese princess tiptoeing through ancient temples in Peking's Forbidden City—they would have, complete with music, sets, costumes, and prewritten dialogue. The Dream Date cassettes would be commercials for sex, love, and more Dream Dates.

Quantril ran a test for his idea on campus, using talent from the film, theater, and communications departments to produce his first video cassette. For the subject of the cassette, he hired a call girl named Wanda Wett to dress up as a medieval damsel performing a slow striptease from the window of a stone tower.

He tried it out on five of the richest guys in school. All five of them were willing to pay four-digit figures for a date with Wanda and the promise of another cassette with an equally scintillating Dream Date.

By the end of his first term, Miles Quantril had made enough money to leave school and head for Hollywood, where he bought up as many cast-off stage sets as he could get hold of. He hired cameramen and directors from porno movies to execute his video extravaganzas. He made commercials of his cassettes and put them on television. Business soared.

Within eight years, Dream Date had branches in fourteen major cities, and the company was grossing in excess of $100 million annually.

Within another four years, Quantril owned controlling shares in more than twenty other companies, and Dream Date expanded to become the core of an international conglomerate spanning the globe.

Within two more years, Quantril was one of the richest men in the world. He had everything he wanted.

Then he got another idea.

It was the same idea Napoleon had had. And Hitler. And Attila the Hun. And Charlemagne.

Miles Quantril intended to control the continent on which he lived. He planned to own the United States of America.

But the new idea required thought. Quantril knew that in a country as stable as the United States, he could never seize control by way of a splashy assassination or a well-armed coup. Nuclear threats were also out of the question. No, he would have to conquer America slowly and subtly, working from the inside out.

It might, he admitted, even take as long as two or three years. But one morning, the country would wake up in Quantril's control without anyone knowing precisely how it happened.

His master plan was centered around a key group of 242 unmarried men. Men who worked in government, banking, transportation, the military, and every other type of big business. All of the carefully selected men worked at the middle management level. They weren't bigwigs, but rather the men who pushed the buttons and filled in the forms, the men who actually did the work necessary to keep America running.

They also all fit into a classic type. They were the kind of guys who, no matter how hard they tried, just couldn't score with women. Quantril had seen thousands of them during the years that Dream Date had been in business. They seemed to share a common leaning toward thick, black-rimmed glasses, plastic pocket pen holders, and bad breath.

Dream Date was the other thing they all had in common.

Quantril used the company to find exactly the right men for his needs.

Dream Date's application forms were changed radically. No other dating service could approach the thoroughness of the Dream Date questionnaires. By the time the applicants were finished with the exhaustive battery of tests and forms, the Dream Date computer knew everything there was to know about them.

The computer had calculated the exact number of men necessary for Quantril's plan to work. It still amazed him that one individual could actually take over a country the size of the United States with the aid of only 242 unwitting accomplices.

He would send them the kinds of women they'd always dreamed of possessing, the kinds of women they could never get on their own. But that was nothing new. The incredibly attractive date was Dream Date's hallmark.

The problem was the women. The call girls and runaways he'd been using would not do for this job. He needed *new* girls, innocents who knew next to nothing. He wanted each of the male applicants his computer had chosen to simply come home from work one evening to find a heavily sedated beauty waiting, stark naked except for a decorative bow and tasteful but anonymous gift card.

According to their psychological profiles, the men would do exactly what Quantril expected them to do: take advantage of the situation. A few days later, when the women started to come out of their drug-induced stupor, Quantril's men would arrive on the scene. They'd come armed with full-color glossies of the debauchery as well as an offer to get rid of the now-enraged women. Quantril figured it would be more than enough to turn each man into a willing cohort in his plan to take over America.

Supplying so many beautiful women had seemed like a real problem at first. But then Quantril realized that kidnaping, like blackmail, could be practiced on a grand scale.

The key word was subtlety. It just wouldn't do to have hordes of screaming women carried off from the same location at the same time. People tended to notice things like that.

He chose instead to let a single man do all the snatching, and that man would never snatch more than two or three women at a time. Quantril had again used Dream Date's files to recruit just the right man for the job. In Wally Donner he recognized a natural predator, a handsome loser fueled by greed. Donner's almost pathological hatred of Mexicans made him perfect. The only thing Quantril had to do was to nudge Donner in the right direction. The man had no more intelligence than a brightly painted windup toy, but once Quantril got him moving, Donner produced a steady stream of dark-eyed beauties from the other side of the border.

As per instructions, Donner delivered each load to an isolated airstrip south of Santa Fe. There the women were picked up and flown to an abandoned monastery in the Sangre de Cristo Mountains. There were more than 180 women up there now, and there was no danger that any of them would escape. A combat-hardened veteran named Deke Bauer saw to that.

Bauer first came to Quantril's attention sometime around the end of the Vietnam War, when Bauer—then an army major—was tried and convicted of war crimes against foreign civilians. During the ensuing flurry of press coverage, it came out that Bauer amused himself during lonely jungle vigils by decapitating young children from both North and South Vietnam. He also mutilated old women, conducted mass hangings of entire villages, and was rumored to have cut off the fingers of the enlisted men under his command when they failed to execute his orders to the letter. Unfortunately, none of the military victims lived to testify against him.

Bauer was Quantril's kind of man. Using the vast resources of Dream Date to bring the major up for retrial and an eventual acquittal, Quantril personally met with Bauer upon his release from the penitentiary.

"What do you know about prisons?" he asked Bauer.

The military man sneered. "They're not so tough."

"Make me one that is," Quantril said. "One that can't be cracked. Ever." Then he took Bauer to the monastery in the mountains.

Bauer was as good as his word. Within a month, he turned the old ruin into an unassailable fortress.

Miles Quantril leaned back in his chair. Today the first of the women was going to be delivered to the first of Quantril's unsuspecting recipients. He smiled at the image his mind conjured up. What would the poor bastard do when he found this unique gift stretched out on his bed?

The phone on the desk purred softly. Quantril slowly crossed the room and lifted the receiver. He didn't bother

46

to say hello. Words like *hello*, *good-bye*, and *thank you* were not part of his vocabulary. Or Deke Bauer's.

"The gift has reached its destination," Bauer said.

Quantril gently replaced the receiver. Feeling a tingle of triumph, he sat down and crossed his legs, taking care not to mar the razor-sharp crease in his trousers. The great game had finally begun. Now it was just a matter of time before it reached its inevitable conclusion.

CHAPTER FOUR

No one knows where the Kanton Indians came from. They simply appeared one day, stepping out of the swirling mists that clung to the upper reaches of the mountain. The first thing their chief did was to borrow a blanket from the startled Hopi shepherd who witnessed their sudden appearance. The chief explained that he hadn't expected it to be terribly cold on the mountain and that he would be sure to return the blanket at first light the next day.

The chief never did get around to returning the blanket. It became the first item in a centuries-long line of unreturned objects and promises postponed for "just another day."

That first night, the Kantons moved into an abandoned campsite and cooked their first meal with pots and food donated by the good-natured Navajo. In the days that followed, it became apparent to all the neighboring tribes that the Kantons had arrived without anything—not even a culture or heritage they could call their own. The Kanton chief kept muttering about "lost baggage" and a great supply of trade goods, precious metals, and gems that were due to arrive in "just another day." But they never did materialize.

So the Kantons kept on borrowing, mainly because the other tribes found it difficult to say no. The Kantons were so charming, so quick to smile and laugh and to break out with the verse and chorus of a recently borrowed song. As the weeks stretched into years, the Kantons continued to raid their neighbors' cultures. Baskets were acquired from the Chacos, weaving and pottery from the Navajo, while the great Anasazi donated an entire pantheon of gods. The Kantons themselves never did much more than sit in the sun. The simple life seemed to suit them, and over the centuries the tribe grew and prospered.

Then one morning the Kantons disappeared as mysteriously as they had come. They were there one moment, and then they were gone, swallowed up by the swirling mountain mists. A few, however, remained behind. There were no more than a half-dozen of the tribe left to carry on the great Kanton traditions. Among that noble six was the woman who would become Sam Wolfshy's great-great-grandmother.

Sam sat on the curb of Harry's Payless service station and garage, tossing pebbles onto the dry ground and occasionally glancing over his shoulder to look at the seatless hull of his jeep.

He was a handsome man in his late twenties. His face

was long and angular, with copper-hued skin stretched taut over jutting cheekbones and a prominent chin. There was a mischievous twinkle in his soft black eyes. Hair of the same color brushed the tops of his shoulders while the rest of it was hidden under a ragged-brimmed straw hat. There'd been no customers for three weeks at Harry's Payless, and Sam was bored. The blood of his Indian ancestors stirred in his veins, but he was helpless to follow his instincts.

Where was the adventure of yesteryear? he wondered. Where were the mountain ponies and the bonfires that crackled on the desert breeze? Sam went into the station, prepared to quit his job to explore the unknown wilderness. His uncle sat behind the counter, reading a newspaper.

"What do you want now, fathead?" his uncle asked.

"Uh, Uncle Harry—"

"Want maybe to quit? Here's your salary." The old man rummaged in the cash register and waved some bills in front of him. "Nice countryside out there. Young man like you could find a job if he wanted to."

Sam swallowed. "Well, actually I was just wondering if I could borrow a Coke."

The hopeful smile on his uncle's face withered as he put the bills back in the register. "No guts," the old man muttered. "You're the damnedest Indian I ever seen. You're dumb, and a coward to boot. You get lost walking around the block. Jesus, a blind man'd be more help around here than you."

"About the Coke, Uncle Harry—"

Harry threw a warm can at his nephew. "Get out of here," he growled.

Sam Wolfshy went back to the curb and sat down. Another attempt at freedom squelched. Ah, well, he reasoned, a guy had to have some loyalty to his family. Especially if they were supporting him. He took a deep drink of the warm soda and closed his eyes. Things weren't so bad, he guessed. It was a good day for working on his tan.

Chiun had not stopped complaining since they left their motel room in Santa Fe.

"Lout. It is an insult."

Remo gripped the wheel of the Chevy until his knuckles turned white. "Little Father, I've already told you a dozen times. We can't wait forever in a motel room. That's not what Smitty sent us here for."

"Imbecile. It is exactly what the Emperor sent us for. If we had waited just a few minutes longer, Mona Madrigal would have come. You have ruined everything."

"For crying out loud, Mona Madrigal doesn't even know we're here."

"Pah. In my village, when a Master of Sinanju appears, the whole village turns out to welcome him."

"Santa Fe's not in Korea."

"The Emperor will be mightily displeased. He sent us to this arid wasteland so that Mona could be presented to me. Now we have insulted his graciousness by leaving so rudely."

"Smitty doesn't even know who Mona Madrigal is," Remo shouted. "There are bodies lying all over the desert—"

52

"A mere ruse," Chiun said with exaggerated patience, wagging his eyebrows up and down. "Can't you see anything? Oh, I should never have accepted a white pupil. You understand nothing."

"I understand that we're supposed to go to the Sangre de Cristo Mountains," Remo said stubbornly. The car produced a series of sputtering, clanking sounds. "That is, if this junk heap will take us there."

With that, there was a scraping sound and then a clunk as the tail pipe clattered to the ground.

"You see?" Chiun grinned in malicious satisfaction.

"See what? I see we lost the freaking tail pipe." As soon as he spoke, two of the hubcaps sprang off the wheels. Remo watched in the rear-view mirror as they spun in lazy circles on the road far behind them.

"See that," Chiun said triumphantly. "This automobile is a sham."

"I can think of other things to call it," Remo said between clenched teeth.

"Emperor Smith never intended for us to drive it. It was part of the pretense. We should have waited in the motel room. The Emperor clearly wished to surprise me."

"Well, he doesn't surprise me. He probably picked up this rattletrap for twenty bucks somewhere, the cheap . . ."

The steering wheel came off in his hands. Seething, Remo tossed it into the back seat. He edged his fingertips into the steering mechanism to maneuver the car as if he were tuning a radio.

Chiun cackled mercilessly. "You see? You should have

listened to me before. Now we must return to the motel. Perhaps Miss Madrigal is already there.''

''Forget it. We're not turning back. All we need is another car.''

The engine sputtered. Remo pumped the gas pedal. The car moved forward erratically.

''I can't believe it,'' Remo said. ''The gas gauge is broken, too. I think we're out of gas.''

Chiun folded his arms over his chest. ''Perhaps you should tell me again, O brilliant one, how necessary this mission is.''

''Can the sarcasm. We're in trouble. Hey, what's that up ahead?'' He squinted. In the distance was a building with two rectangular objects in front of it. ''I'll be damned,'' Remo said, visibly relieved. ''A gas station. I guess we're in luck after all.''

''What great good fortune,'' Chiun muttered.

A dark-haired young man leaped up when Remo pulled into Harry's Payless.

''Hey, nice car you got,'' he said, reaching in and fingering the upholstery.

Remo slapped his hands away in annoyance. ''Do you mind? Just fill it up.''

''Okay,'' the young man said affably. ''Just taking a look, that's all. Say, you got a smoke?''

''No,'' Remo said. ''Is there a used-car lot around here?''

''Nothing close. You know you got no steering wheel?''

''That's a real eagle eye you have,'' Remo said.

''I can fix it. Good as new. Only take a sec.''

Remo looked at the young man. He seemed friendly enough. "Are you a mechanic?"

"I'm an Indian," the young man said proudly. "Sam Wolfshy. Got a stick of gum?"

"No," Remo said, exasperated.

"How about a couple of rubber bands?"

"What for?"

Wolfshy shrugged. "They're useful. Can't tell when you'll need one."

"I don't have anything except money," Remo said.

"Oh." The Indian looked down, disinterested.

"I'd like to buy a map."

"Inside," Wolfshy said. "Harry'll help you."

"I'll go with you," Chiun said. "These gasoline fumes are assaulting my nostrils." He got out of the car. "I will probably be dead of poison fumes before dawn," the Oriental droned. "Dead, without ever having met Mona Madrigal. The Emperor's gracious present will have gone to waste. Of course, returning to our motel might save my life. But don't consider me, Remo. What is the life of an old man?"

"That's big of you, Chiun," Remo said, striding into the station.

Behind the counter sat a skinny old man with arms like toasted bread sticks, reading a newspaper. He wore a bright flowered shirt and thick glasses that had slid down to the base of his nose.

"Ice machine's broken," he said, glancing up at Remo. "Won't be fixed before tomorrow." He gave his paper a shake and went back to reading it.

55

"I'm not here for ice. I need a map."

"No maps. Sam borrowed them all."

"What's he want them for?"

"Who knows? He's a Kanton."

Remo shook his head. "I think I missed something there."

"Forget it. Anything else?"

"I need another car."

"Can't help you there," Harry said, turning a page of the newspaper. "Closest car dealer's back in Santa Fe."

"You see?" Chiun hissed. "It's fate."

"How far is it to the Sangre de Cristo Mountains?"

Harry squinted toward the fluorescent ceiling lights. "Can't say. Never been there. Sam might know. He's a Kanton."

"You've said that before. What the hell's a Kanton?"

"Indian, son. They come from around the Sangre de Cristo." Suddenly the old man grinned. He slapped his newspaper down so hard that his glasses slid off his nose. "You know what you need?"

"Yes," Remo said. "A map."

"Better'n that. You need a guide. A real wood-tracking, wind-smelling Indian guide. And I got just the man for you."

"Sam?" Remo asked without enthusiasm.

"None other." Harry slapped his knee and chuckled.

'Uh, no thanks," Remo said. "I think you need him more here."

"Hell, no. What I mean is," he added quickly, "it's the slow season. I can spare him for a few days. Come on,

56

mister. What do you say?'' There was pleading in his eyes.

Remo looked at him suspiciously. ''I think I'll pass on Sam.''

The old man exhaled noisily. ''Shit,'' he said. ''I didn't think it would work. Fact is, he's my nephew. My sister married a Kanton, and when she passed on, I got saddled with Sam. That was twenty-six years ago. Haven't been able to get rid of him since.''

''What's wrong with him?''

''He's a damned Kanton, that's what's wrong,'' Harry screeched. ''They're borrowers. They can't help it. It's in their blood. But it's driving me crazy. Got a shirt? Got a vacuum cleaner bag? Sheesh. Ever see the Kanton Indian Museum? It's got nothing but I.O.U.'s in it, some going back to the sixteen hundreds.''

''You mean Sam's a thief?''

''Hell, no,'' Harry said, waving his hand. ''Couldn't care less about money. Don't own anything, don't want to. But he'll borrow the teeth out of your head.''

''Well, we don't have anything to borrow,'' Remo said, considering. ''And we could use a guide, I suppose. . . .''

''I'll tell you what,'' Harry interjected. ''You take Sam off my hands, and the gas you got's on the house.''

''Gee, I don't know—''

''We accept,'' Chiun said.

''We-ha!'' Harry whooped, scurrying from behind the counter. ''I'll tell Sam to get ready.''

When the old man had run out, Remo turned to Chiun. ''What'd you say that for? We don't even know this guy.''

Chiun folded his hands into his sleeves. "It is simple. Now we have free gas. With it, we can return to Santa Fe. We will offer up this Sam person to the Emperor, saying that he forced us to leave our motel room temporarily. That way, Emperor Smith will not be offended that we were not present to receive a visit from Mona Madrigal."

Remo knocked the heel of his hand against his temple. "Are you kidding? That's the most twisted argument I've ever heard."

"With emperors, subtlety is everything," Chiun assured him.

A shriek that sounded like a strangled vulture sent them running outside.

It was Sam Wolfshy. He was lying on the ground, legs sprawled, arms flailing, his tongue hanging out of his mouth as Harry squeezed his neck with both scrawny hands.

"What's going on here?" Remo asked, pulling the old man off the big Indian. "I thought you liked him."

"Damned worthless Kanton!" Harry screeched. "I lay my balls on the line to give you a chance with these guys, and look what you do to their car!"

"Car?" Remo asked. He looked around for the Chevy. It was parked beside a jeep.

"I fixed the steering wheel, didn't I?" Sam protested.

Remo looked inside the car with amazement. Indeed, the steering wheel was back in place. But both seats, as well as the dashboard, radio, cigarette lighter, windshield wipers, door handles, rear-view mirror, and all four tires were gone. They had all been neatly installed in the jeep next to it.

"He works quickly," Chiun said, impressed.

"So will the police," Remo said, turning to Wolfshy.

The Indian blinked in bewilderment. "But I only borrowed those accessories."

Harry clasped both hands to his head and reeled inside.

"Accessories?" Remo shouted. "You call tires accessories?"

"Hold, hold," Chiun said. "This person has possibilities."

"So do a lot of guys in San Quentin."

"Use your head, Remo. We take *his* car."

Remo looked from the old Oriental to the jeep. "Not bad, Little Father."

"Hey, wait a minute," Sam waffled. "I don't know about that."

"Let me explain it to you," Remo said in the manner of a born teacher. "Either we take your jeep, or you spend the next couple of years in the state pen. Now, what's your answer?"

Wolfshy looked blankly at Remo for a moment, then broke into a broad grin. "Looks like you two just hired yourselves a genuine Indian guide." He held out his hand.

Remo ignored it and pointed to the jeep. "You drive," he said.

Wolfshy climbed in. "We'll be able to drive to the foothills of the Sangre de Cristos, but then we'll have to walk," he said cheerfully.

"So you've been to the mountains before?"

"Not really," Wolfshy said. "A hiker told me a couple of months ago. Loaned me these boots I'm wearing."

"That figures," Remo said.

Wolfshy continued, undaunted, "Nice guy. Said he went to check out an old Franciscan monastery at the top of one of the peaks, but when he got there, the place was swarming with soldiers. They chased him off."

"American soldiers?"

"I guess. He didn't say." Wolfshy revved up the engine.

"Hold it," Remo said. "I need to make a phone call."

Inside the station, Harry was beaming. "So you're going to take him after all, are you?"

"Yeah. Where's the phone?"

Harry pointed.

"Do me a favor, will you, and clear out for a couple of minutes? This call's private."

"Sure." Harry gave him a lewd wink. "Got a little honey, eh?"

Remo thought of Harold W. Smith's pinched, lemony face. "Not exactly," he said.

Smith's computers whirred and beeped for less than twenty seconds before Remo got his answer. "There's no American military base in the Sangre de Cristo Mountains," the lemony voice said.

"That's all I wanted to know," Remo said, and hung up. He climbed into the jeep. "We're going to that monastery. Which way is it?"

"Due north," Wolfshy said with authority.

Jubilantly, Harry waved good-bye to them as Wolfshy turned a slow circle in front of the gas station.

Remo relaxed. "I guess it's a good thing we've got you along after all," he said to the Indian. "I'd hate to get lost in those mountains."

Wolfshy turned another circle, and then went around a third time.

"Think we can stop the parade and get going?" Remo snapped.

"Sure," Wolfshy said. "There's just one thing."

"What is it?"

"Which way is north?"

CHAPTER FIVE

The petite blonde clutched at her stomach and moaned. "I need a doctor," she pleaded through clenched teeth. "You've got to help me. I think it's my appendix."

She was about to say something more, but instead she drew a sharp breath, doubling over with pain.

The other women stirred to life. During the day, the former chapel let in light from its high windows, revealing the monastery's adobe walls and filthy stone floor. The women huddled together in the corners for warmth, their faces gray, their expressions numb and blank. Some of them bore fresh wounds from the beatings they received from the guards.

Consuela Madera went to the blonde girl. They had awakened together, along with Consuela's sisters, in this damp, terrifying place. When the Madera girls learned that their parents and brother were gone, probably dead, the younger girls became hysterical with grief. Their wails brought the guards who brought their sticks and fists.

Consuela learned quickly to put her own fear aside to help the others. As if sharing an unspoken communication with the beautiful Mexican woman, the young blonde named Karen joined her in nursing the sick and comforting the despairing among them. From their first days together, Karen and Consuela had become the kind of friends who would do anything for one another without question.

"What is wrong, Karen?" Consuela wrapped her arms around the blonde, leading her toward the wall. "How can I help?"

"I'm all right," Karen whispered. "Just go along. Try to get a guard in here."

Consuela obeyed without hesitation. "Guard!" she shouted. "We need a doctor. This woman is very sick."

Karen moaned. Clutching at the folds of her shapeless gray gown, she slumped against the wall and slid to the floor, her head tossing from side to side. "Help me," she screamed. "I'm burning up inside."

Finally Karen heard the sounds of motion overhead, the scraping noise of a chair being shoved back, the thud of boots on a tile floor, and then after a moment's silence, the metallic snick of a key turning in a lock. She drew a deep breath as the big oak door creaked on its hinges. *He's coming*, she thought. *He really is coming.*

The small blonde kept her head down as the heavy-footed guard made his way across to where she was resting against the rough adobe wall. The other women moved out of his path, sticking in small groups. Consuela recited a prayer.

The guard, a young, dull-looking man named Kains, hesitated as he passed the Mexican girl. Unconsciously his tongue slid over his lips.

She's so beautiful, he thought. His spark-less eyes ceased to blink as his gaze rested on Consuela's buttocks. His hand reached out to touch her, but he pulled back. *No. She's different from the others.*

Consuela had been the only one of the new arrivals to look him in the eye. Without fear, she had demanded bandages and water for the others. And when he had brought them water, Consuela thanked him. *She's a real lady*, Kains thought.

Not like this other pain in the ass who was always causing problems. "What's wrong with you?" Kains asked harshly, stepping toward the shivering blonde on the floor.

"I'm sick," Karen gasped.

Scowling, Kains tugged at his peak-billed cap. Well," he muttered, "we ain't got a doctor." His deep-set eyes mirrored uncertainty. "One of the guards used to be a medic, though. Maybe he'll take a look at you."

"Oh, God," Karen moaned. She reached out and grabbed Kains's arm as if to steady herself. The gesture forced the guard to move in closer or lose his balance. His booted feet shifted. The butt of his shoulder-slung rifle jabbed into his back.

"Screw you," Karen whispered. Using the wall for support, she brought up her knee, driving it into Kains's unprotected groin. The startled guard let out a whoosh of air like a punctured bellows. He doubled over, clutching at his manhood while Consuela jumped on his back, wrapping her thin arms around Kains's bull neck.

"Get his gun," Karen shouted. She pushed off the wall again, ramming her head into the wide, soft target of the guard's stomach. Kains made a dry, retching sound and wobbled, but he managed to stay on his feet. He cocked his balled fist back and slammed it down into the little blonde's mouth.

Consuela screamed as Karen slumped to the floor, a spray of blood shooting from her nose. Overhead, a staccato burst of automatic fire stitched a ragged line across the wall. The noise was deafening, but the weapons were aimed too high to actually hit the women. Loosened clay dust swirled in the air. There were screams, muttered curses, and a thrashing of limbs as the panicked women scrambled for cover.

"It's over now," a deep voice bellowed. "Everybody calm down and you won't be hurt."

Karen peeked cautiously up at the man in the overhead gallery. His machine gun was still cradled in his arms, but the barrel was pointing skyward as if he were certain he wouldn't have to use it. The smoldering butt of a cigarette dangled from the corner of his mouth. He hadn't even bothered to put it out.

This is all in a day's work for them, Karen realized. They'd known from the beginning that she and Consuela and the other women didn't have a prayer of overpowering the guards in this nightmarish asylum.

"Let this be a lesson to you," the stern voice continued

from above. "There's no way out of here until we decide to let you go. Try something stupid like that again, girlies, and there won't be enough coffins around here to handle all of you."

Dumb bastard, Karen brooded. She'd "girlie" him. One day.

She put her hand to her face. Her front teeth ached but were not broken. Kains, a few feet away, brushed off his clothes and readjusted his peaked cap at a rakish angle.

"Lying bitch," he muttered. He glared down at Karen, spun around, and stomped out of the room. She couldn't help smiling when she noticed that his gait was a little lopsided.

Consuela knelt beside her. "Are you hurt?" she asked gently.

"Nothing's broken."

"You were lucky. This time. Don't try such a crazy thing again, Karen."

"I've got to get out of here," the blonde said stubbornly.

"We all want to leave."

"Maybe so. But I'm going to."

Consuela sighed. "Then at least use your head. One woman cannot punch and kick her way out of this place. You need more than courage."

Karen smiled bitterly. "What else have I got?"

"You need a plan."

"Such as what?" She gestured toward the vaulted ceiling and high, slitlike windows. "There's no way out of here except through the door."

"Is that so?" Consuela said abstractedly, looking from

67

the high windows to Karen. "You seem to be quick and agile. Are you an athlete?"

Karen grinned. "State gymnastics champion," she said. "But that was back in high school. I haven't competed in two years."

"Can you fit through that window?"

Karen tried to judge the width of the opening. "I think so," she said. "But how would I get up there? We haven't got any rope."

"Our gowns," Consuela said, beaming. "Each of us will tear four inches off the bottom. If we all do it, the guards won't notice. We'll knot the pieces into a rope."

Karen touched Consuela's arm. "Thanks for trying to help. But tying these rags together isn't going to do anything. I'd need something to hook onto the window. A spike, a broom handle—something solid. We haven't got anything like that."

"What about this?" Looking around briefly, she reached under her shift and pulled out a wooden billy club.

"Consuela! How'd you—"

"It's Kains's. He's on lunch break. He won't miss it for a while."

"But how—"

The Mexican woman laughed. "I took it while they were all busy with you," she said. "But we must act quickly. Kains will come back for it soon."

"What'll he do to you when he finds out?"

"Probably nothing," Consuela said casually. "He likes me. I can tell. Don't worry about me. Just get some help

and come back as fast as you can with the police, okay?''
She tore the hem of her dress. ''Hurry.''

Karen tore her own gown and knotted the pieces together as Consuela gathered pieces of material from the
other women.

In a few minutes, the makeshift rope was ready. Karen
tied it to the billy club and flung it toward the window
high overhead. The club fell short, clattering to the floor.
Instinctively the women turned toward the big oak door
that separated them from the guards. It did not open.

Karen tried again, and a third time. On the fourth try,
the club sailed through the open slit in the wall. There
was an audible sigh from everyone in the area.

''Quick! Someone's coming!''

Clenching her jaw, trying to remain calm, Karen patiently climbed the rope. Her palms were sweating and her
shoulders ached, but she kept moving, hand over hand, her
feet braced against the wall.

''Hurry!'' Consuela hissed.

With a huge effort, Karen threw one leg through the
window. Then, straddling the opening, she reversed the
guard's nightstick to the interior wall and pulled the makeshift rope out.

When Kains and another guard arrived, the only trace of
Karen Lockwood was the nightstick jammed horizontally
against the slitted window.

''What's going on here?'' Kains demanded, fixing the
women with his beast's stare.

Consuela stepped forward. Swallowing the lump in her
throat, she forced herself to smile. ''We are pleased you

have come, señor," she said. As if by accident, the sleeve of her gown slipped off her left shoulder, revealing a rounded portion of her ample breasts. Kains gaped at her. She could see his breathing coming heavily.

The moment was broken by the sound of the nightstick clattering to the floor. Behind it flew the stream of rags used to make a rope. Karen had escaped.

"Hey, what's that?" the guard with Kains asked.

Kains picked it up, then felt the empty leather loop on his belt. "It's my club," he said, puzzled. "I didn't know it was gone."

"These bitches did it," the other guard muttered. He pointed at the crowd of prisoners as he counted. "One short," he said, and pressed a button near the big oak door. A loud, whopping alarm sounded, followed by the stamping of feet as the prison guards systematically searched the area for escapees. "The snotty little blonde got out," the guard said. He grabbed Consuela by the arm. "Where'd she go?"

Kains pushed him away. "What're you picking on her for?"

"They're thick as thieves, those two. The Mex bitch knows where the other one went." He turned to Consuela. "Don't you, bitch?" he slapped her hard across the face. "I asked you a question." He slapped her again. A trickle of blood appeared at the corner of her lips.

Kains raised his nightstick over the other guard. "Cut it out!" he shouted. His eyes were wild.

"Hey, what's the matter? You got the hots for the broad or what?"

Kains was about to strike him when the big oak door opened and a double line of uniformed men strode in. Between them marched a man in his forties wearing a crisp black uniform with a major's insignia borrowed from the U.S. Army. He was tough looking and mean, with the kind of clean, humorless face that seemed to be reserved for religious fanatics and professional military officers.

Kains dropped the club to salute the superior officer.

"How'd it happen?" the major snapped.

"Looks like she went through the window, sir," Kains answered. "Made a rope out of scraps of cloth, sir."

The major took in the information, his face bitter as he surveyed the hint of triumph on the expressions of the prisoners. He jerked his head toward Consuela Madera. "Why is her face bloody?" he demanded.

The guard with Kains spoke. "She's a friend of the prisoner who escaped, sir. Thought we'd get her to talk."

"About what?" the major sneered. "They don't even know where they are. Fool. You've bruised her face for nothing."

"I'm sorry, sir."

"What's your name, soldier?"

"Dexter, sir. Corporal Robert T."

"You're not here to damage the goods, Dexter."

"No, sir."

"No matter what kind of trouble they cause, you don't go around hitting a woman in the mouth, is that clear?"

"Yes, sir."

"You hit them in the body, like this," the major said, demonstrating with a powerful right hook to Consuela's

71

abdomen. The woman moaned, her head snapping back as she folded forward with the pain.

Major Deke Bauer brushed his hands together. "That way, they still look good. Understand?"

"Yes, sir," Dexter said.

"By the way, were you two on duty during the escape?"

"Sort of, sir. We were on our lunch break—"

"That's all right, corporal."

Dexter's haggard face relaxed. "Thank you, sir."

Bauer took out his revolver, a Colt Magnum. "Think nothing of it," he said, and fired point blank into the man's face.

When his body with its still-surprised eyes hit the floor, Bauer kicked it toward Kains. "See that this doesn't happen again," the major said in a quiet voice before he left.

Kains felt the blood drain from his face. As he followed Bauer and his men out, he stole a glance at Consuela. She was on her hands and knees on the floor beside Dexter's body. Her head sagged as she tried to raise herself up, Kains wished he could help her. But he knew he was no match for Deke Bauer.

A half-hour later, Bauer sat with his feet propped up on a paper-littered rolltop desk. He took a long pull at his dappled green cigar while, in the distance, the sharp explosive bark of a machine gun punctuated the still afternoon.

His men hadn't caught up with the Lockwood girl yet, but it wouldn't be long. No unarmed female could hide in these mountains for long. Her escape was a minor slipup, nothing to worry about. He blew a spiral of smoke toward the ceiling. A smile played at the corners of his hard-set mouth. Only a very few things elicited a smile from him. The sound of gunfire was one of them.

Swinging his legs off the desk, he crossed to where a fire of piñon logs blazed in the fieldstone hearth. He picked up a poker and idly probed the blaze, setting off a shower of sparks. The sight reminded him of artillery flares. The corners of his mouth went up. Artillery flares were another thing that made the major smile.

On the whole, he felt damn good about having his own command again. True, it was only fifty men, but among them were some of the best combat soldiers to come out of Nam. Bauer himself had whipped them back into shape with an entire month of intensive retraining. They were well armed, well paid, and ready for anything that might come their way.

So far nothing had. The girl's feeble attempt at escape wasn't even worth a thought, as far as Bauer was concerned. His men would test themselves against real fighting men when the time came. Miles Quantril had promised him that chance, and Bauer trusted him, in a perverse kind of way. Despite Quantril's cruelty, there was something almost military in the man's bearing and in the way his voice carried the weight of authority.

Bauer turned away from the fireplace and ran his hand along a shelf of war mementos near his desk. There were his medals, of course. Twelve of them in two neat rows, pinned on a field of deep blue velvet. Next to them was an assortment of newspaper clippings and telegrams, yellowing now in their carefully dusted frames. The clippings were all about the war. He'd thrown out all the stories about his trial, treating them like the garbage they were. Candy-ass civilians, he'd thought. They don't know what war's like.

Deke Bauer knew. War was excitement. It was challenge. It was the only real test of a man's worth. War was life.

The last item on the shelf was a fading snapshot of a much younger Bauer, standing in a jungle clearing with three other men, all in uniform. He couldn't remember the occasion for the picture, but it must have been something special, because all three of the men in the photo were enlisted men under him, and he'd never particularly liked any of them. Still, it was the only picture of Bauer from the war that had survived, and so it had taken on a special importance for him.

"Tabert, Hancock, and Williams," the major muttered to himself. Hancock had bought the farm three days after the picture had been taken. Bauer had no idea what had happened to Tabert. He'd read something about Williams years ago. He'd become a cop or something. Then he went bad and ended up going to the electric chair.

It came as no surprise to Bauer. There'd always been something not quite right about Williams.

There was a sharp rap at the door. Like everyone else in Bauer's outfit, the sergeant at the threshold was dressed in black. An Uzi submachine gun was slung over his shoulder.

"We've spotted the prisoner, sir," he said.

"Has she been stopped?"

"No, sir. She's keeping close to rocks and vegetation, sir. But she's headed down the south side of the mountain.

It looks like she's going to run right into a carload of intruders, sir.''

"Intruders?"

"Three men, sir. One of them's an old Oriental. They're about halfway up the mountain.''

"Campers?"

"Probably, sir.''

The major nodded thoughtfully. "Take a team of eight men and eliminate them. And the girl. Bring the bodies back here. Understand, Sergeant Brickell?''

Brickell understood. He understood that if he didn't bring the bodies back, he didn't have to bother to come back himself.

As he hurried out of the room, Bauer smiled again. Death was one of those things that always made him smile.

CHAPTER SIX

At 6,000 feet, the juniper and sagebrush of the Sangre de Cristos gave way to towering Douglas firs and thick stands of ponderosa pine.

Sam Wolfshy gunned the jeep's engine, but the wheels only spun helplessly on the steep, rocky incline.

"It's no use," Remo said. "We'd better get out and walk."

"Walk? What'll happen to my jeep if we leave it here?" Wolfshy protested.

"This is the middle of nowhere. Besides, you said yourself that we'd have to leave it."

"Not in the middle of nowhere! How'll we ever find it again?"

"That's your problem," Remo said irritably. "You're supposed to be the great Indian guide."

"I am," Sam protested. "I am a full-blooded Kanton."

His eyes hardened with inner conviction. "These mountains are the hunting grounds of my ancestors. Through my veins—"

"Oh, bulldookey," Remo said. "Since we left Harry's gas station, we've gotten lost eight times."

"I can't help if it the moss grows on the wrong side of the trees here."

"Moss always grows on the north side."

"Only white man's moss," Wolfshy said with dignity.

Remo sighed and started up the hill. It was nearly sunset, and the shadows were deepening. The temperature at the high elevation was considerably colder than it had been in the sun-washed foothills.

Behind him Chiun walked regally through the dense forest, his blue robe fluttering in the breeze. Sam Wolfshy was still back at the car, struggling to strap a knapsack full of provisions onto his back.

"Which path do we take?" Remo called from a granite outcropping beside a fork in the trail.

"Uh, left," Sam said. "No, I think we ought to go right. Well, actually there's something to be said for both directions."

"You're the most indecisive human being I've ever met!" Remo exploded.

"I'm just open-minded," the Indian said, hurt.

"Don't you have a map?"

"I don't need a map. I'm a full-blooded Kanton."

Remo sputtered, then forced himself to calm down. "All right, Sam. Have it your way. But if we get lost again, I'm going to see to it that you're not a full-blooded anything, got it?''

"Well, I do happen to have a little map," Wolfshy said, reaching into his coat. "Harry was kind enough to loan it to me."

Remo snatched it from him. "This is a road map," he yelled. "What good is this going to do us? The nearest road is twenty miles away."

"There are things on here besides roads. Look." Wolfshy pointed to a pink splotch. "Here are the Sangre de Cristo Mountains. That's where we are."

"No kidding," Remo said, crumpling the map into a ball and throwing it as far as he could. "It's already getting dark. We'll never find our way to the monastery before tomorrow."

"Look, why don't we just make the best of things?" Wolfshy suggested. "We're in a kind of clearing here. I'll build a fire and cook up some supper. Then, after a good night's rest, we can make our way to the top of the range tomorrow. We won't have to go up much farther before we can see the mission." He smiled. "How does that sound?"

"Do you always have to be so damned cheerful?" Remo growled. "It's getting on my nerves."

"Sorry." Wolfshy arranged some sticks inside a circle of stones for a fire. "Say, could I borrow a match?"

Without speaking, Remo picked up a small gray stone and spun it toward the unlit fire. The stone first struck one rock, then the second and third, and continued around the circle, sending off shooting sparks each time it struck. The movement was so fast that, to Sam Wolfshy, the fire seemed to ignite spontaneously.

"Wow, that was really something," he said. "Maybe you're part Indian. Do you think I could learn that? I mean, it must be in my blood, right? I could—"

Inexplicably, he turned a double back flip, then landed in a sitting position.

Chiun was standing nearby, slapping his hands together as if to wipe dust from them. The expression on his face was sour. "Keep this person out of my sight," he said.

"He doesn't mean any harm," Remo whispered. "And we did ask him to be our guide."

"Guide? Hah. This mushroom-brained fool is incapable of guiding himself across a postage stamp. Also, he talks incessantly. He has no sense of direction. He is a stone around our necks. And today alone, he has asked to borrow sixty-four items from me."

"Yeah, he's a dipstick," Remo said. He looked past Chiun to the fire, where Wolfshy crouched, stirring the contents of a metal pot with a stick and singing "Old MacDonald," complete with sound effects, at the top of his voice. "But there's something about him I kind of like."

Wolfshy looked up and smiled. "Chow's ready," he called.

"At least he can cook," Remo said. With a snort, Chiun padded to the fire.

"Hope you guys are hungry," Wolfshy said, sniffing the air like some TV-show gourmet. "Doesn't that smell good?"

"What manner of foulness is that?" Chiun shrieked, pointing to the pot.

Wolfshy looked into the pot, then at Chiun, then back at the pot. "Beans," he said innocently. "Just baked beans. Very nourishing, if you don't mind a little gas."

"And those globs of fat?" The old man's long fingers quivered over the bubbling concoction.

"That's pork. It gives the beans more flavor. Here, have a taste."

Chiun slapped the stick out of the Indian's hand. "Remo, eliminate him."

"Calm down, Chiun," Remo said. "He was only—"

"Not only is he a brainless, worthless fool, but now he seeks to poison the Master of Sinanju by feeding him pork fat."

"Gosh, I wasn't . . ."

Remo silenced him with a gesture. He listened to the forest. There was a sound that did not belong.

Immediately, Chiun and Remo went to opposite sides of the clearing, and it came again: a faint rustle of leaves and the unmistakable crack of wood beneath a human foot.

Silently Remo darted into the forest. There was a flutter of activity and a muffled cry. When he reappeared, he was holding a small, dirty, unconscious woman in his arms.

"Who's that?" Wolfshy asked.

Remo set her on the ground. "How would I know? She tripped and knocked herself on the head before I could reach her."

"The garment she is wearing is disgusting," Chiun said, wrinkling his nose. "Perhaps she is a musician."

The woman groaned as she came to. As soon as she saw their faces, she flailed out with both her fists.

"Take it easy," Remo said, catching her hands in one of his. "Nobody's going to hurt you."

She looked around, her eyes wide and frightened. "You're not with them?" she whispered.

"Whoever 'they' are, we're not. You're safe."

"Thank God." She buried her face in Remo's chest and sobbed. "I made it. I got away."

Remo rocked her gently. Wherever she had been, it obviously hadn't been a picnic for her. "Can you tell me about it?"

"Yes . . . that's why I'm here," she said, sniffing. "I've got to get help. For the others."

"Slow down," Remo said. "What others? Where did you come from?"

The woman clasped her hands together in an effort to calm herself. "My name is Karen Lockwood," she said shakily. She told them about the strange occurrences that had taken place since she'd been picked up by a blue Econoline van off the interstate.

"The prison's on this mountain?"

Karen nodded. "I think it used to be a church or something. While I was running away from the place, I looked back and saw a bell tower."

"Sounds like the Franciscan monastery," Wolfshy said.

"Well, there aren't any Franciscans there now. Those soldiers shot at me every step of the way until it got dark."

Chiun's brow creased. "Then they are nearby."

"We've all got to get out of here and contact the police," Karen said. "How far is the nearest town?"

"It's fifty miles or so to Santa Fe. You can take the jeep. We'll stay on here," Remo said.

"Uh, are you sure about that?" Sam sputtered. "I mean, if they've got guns and everything—"

"All right, you can go with the girl."

Sam's pinched face relaxed. "I'll take good care of her, don't you worry. Why, when my ancestors walked this land—"

"Shhh." Remo nodded toward Karen. She was propped up beside a rock, fast asleep. Her dirty face looked as innocent as a child's.

"She was exhausted," Chiun said. "Let her sleep. There will be time in the morning to go for the police."

"And easier to find our way, too," Wolfshy added.

Remo cast him a withering look.

"Well, anyone can get lost."

"Go to sleep," Remo said.

"What about those soldiers she was talking about?"

"They've probably given up the search. At least for tonight. I'll wake you if anybody comes."

"Aren't you going to sleep?"

"Not if you two continue this offensive chatter," Chiun screeched from the other side of the clearing. He was sitting in full lotus beneath a tree.

"Sorry," Wolfshy said. "I didn't know you were asleep. Your eyes were open. I guess that's Zen, huh? Like hearing the sound of one hand clapping." Sam grinned, pleased with himself.

"If you are not utterly silent within five seconds," Chiun said, "you will hear the sound of one hand tearing the tongue from your throat."

Wolfshy walked wordlessly to his sleeping bag. Remo took it from him. "For the girl," he whispered. The Indian curled near the dying fire as Remo carried the sleeping woman to the warm pallet.

The night was silent except for the chattering of small woodland animals. Remo lay beside Karen Lockwood, studying her face. It was bruised and cut, and her arms bore marks of beatings. What had she been through? What sort of men ran the prison at the top of the hill, and why?

Karen had said that all the prisoners were young women who'd been kidnaped. They believed their families had been destroyed. That had to account for the bodies found in the mesa, Remo figured. So the rash of unexplained murders Smith was so concerned about was only the beginning.

Remo looked through the woods up the rocky slope of the mountain. Somewhere atop that peak stood a fortress where a madman kept a harem of beautiful women, and then tortured and starved them. Whoever that man was, Remo was going to find him. As soon as the girl and the Indian were out of the way, Remo and Chiun would begin the search.

A twig snapped. From the lightness of the sound, Remo knew a man hadn't caused it, but Karen was up like a bolt, eyes wide open, mouth gasping in fear.

"It's all right," Remo said gently.

She pumped her legs out of her sleeping bag, oblivious to his reassurances. "They're coming," she said.

"No, they're not. Honest. It's just an animal or something."

Sweat was pouring down her face. Remo knew nothing would calm her now except hard evidence. "Look. I'll prove it, okay?"

He stalked silently into the woods. Karen listened. The young man with the thick wrists made no sound as he walked. Then a tree shuddered and there was a sudden commotion that made her feel as if her heart had just shot into her throat. A moment later, something came hurtling out of the shadows at her.

Karen screamed.

In a split second, Chiun was on his feet, in fighting position.

"Wazzat?" Sam Wolfshy said, blinking and snorting.

"A raccoon," Remo called, stepping out of the woods. "That's all it was, Karen. Just a raccoon."

As he spoke, a frightened, black-masked creature scuttled across the clearing and darted down the footpath.

"You have awakened me for a raccoon?" Chiun shouted.

"I'm sorry," Remo said. "Karen was afraid—"

"Silence!"

"Hey, what's going on?" Sam said, rubbing his eyes. "I heard . . . oof." He slid bonelessly down the trunk of a tree.

"Do you wish to speak again?" Chiun bellowed.

Sam shook his head earnestly.

"Then perhaps now we may get some rest." The

old Oriental floated to the ground and resumed his lotus position.

"Come on," Remo said softly. He put his arm around Karen and led her back to her sleeping bag.

"I'm sorry," she said. "Guess I was just jumpy." A tear ran down her cheek.

"Don't cry," Remo said. "I can't take it."

"Oh, God. I don't even know why I'm crying. I'm just tired, I guess, and scared, and I've got to get the police, and there are over a hundred people trapped up there, and a bunch of idiots have been trying to kill me all day. . . ." She covered her face with her hands.

"Come on," Remo said, holding her. "That's too much for one person to handle all at once. Just try to forget about it for a minute, okay?"

"I can't forget. I've got to . . ." Involuntarily she sipped a mouthful of air as Remo's fingers played on her shoulders. Their grip was delicate and tentative at first, then grew stronger as they began to work away the tension that gripped her body. There was something soothing and comforting in the motion of his hands. Karen felt her stomach unknot. She felt a warm glow, first of contentment, then of desire.

She wound her arms around Remo's neck. Their lips brushed together, and she felt as if a flash fire were consuming her. She murmured a few incoherent words before the animal part of her mind blocked out all the useless thoughts that kept her away from the man who was bringing her senses to life. There would be no more thinking. Her body had taken over. A spirit flying free for the first time, her desire had its way. In Remo's arms she felt as free as a bird, soaring and diving among the clouds.

Spent, she slept in his arms. She was small, and to Remo she felt as light as a little girl.

Then another twig snapped.

"What was that?" Karen gasped, immediately awake.

"Now, don't start that again." Remo held her tightly.

"But I heard something."

"So did I. It's probably just another raccoon."

"Or something larger," Chiun said, rising as if he were floating off the ground.

"Will you cut it out? She's scared enough," Remo said.

"I will see." The old Oriental walked softly across the clearing.

"Freeze it right there, slope."

Remo and Chiun turned toward the source of the unfamiliar voice. When a man clad in black stepped into the clearing, Karen screamed. "It's them," she squeaked. Her hands shook violently.

The soldier was big, bigger than Remo, with powerful shoulders and a broad, craggy face. The Uzi submachine gun he was holding was pointed directly at Chiun.

Out of the corner of his eye, Remo saw seven more men fan out around the campsite. They were dressed in black as well, each one carrying a snub-nosed Uzi. They moved well, as if accustomed to the mechanics of ambush. Silently they formed a wide circle around the four civilians, sealing off all exits.

Remo glanced over at Wolfshy. The Indian groaned

once in his sleep, turned, and opened his eyes groggily. "Hey, what—"

One of the soldiers thrust his weapon toward Wolfshy's face. Wolfshy sprang backward on his elbows with a yelp.

"Take it easy, Sam," Remo said quietly. He didn't move a muscle. "What do you want?" he asked the soldiers.

"The girl. Hand her over."

"You—you can't do that," Wolfshy stammered.

"Shut up, jerk. If I want any shit, I'll squeeze your head." He raised the Uzi into firing position. "The girl. Now. Otherwise the old gook gets it between the eyes."

"She is not yours to take," Chiun said.

"Oh, no?" The team leader's eyes shone with amused malice in the moonlight. "Just watch me."

He began to squeeze the trigger. Then, suddenly, the weapon was no longer in his hands. The frail-looking old man was beside him. The soldier felt his body being lifted in the air. A moment later, a wave of pain engulfed him, and then there was nothing. His lifeless body slid down the granite wall against which it had been crushed.

The other soldiers were still for a moment, unable to believe what they'd just seen. But they were well trained, and their reflexes were fast. The soldier nearest Wolfshy spun to fire at the Indian's head.

Remo saw the beginning of the movement as soon as the soldier's feet started to turn. He leaped diagonally toward him, feet first, and landed square in the man's chest. The weapon clattered against the trunk of a tree as a bright spurt of blood shot from his mouth.

In the same motion, Remo grabbed Sam Wolfshy and tossed him into the air, out of the line of fire. The startled Indian grasped a large branch and scurried to safety near the trunk.

Another of the soldiers came after the girl. He had her by her hair when a thin, yellowed hand with long fingernails slashed across his face. He shouted in pain, his hands covering the bloody blankness that used to be his eyes. With another razor blow from Chiun's delicate hands, the man was dead.

The others ran. They knew the woods, but Remo was faster than they were, and his vision was better. Within seconds he'd broken the back of one of the men and smashed the skulls of two more. He heard a sound and, turning, saw Chiun behind him, delivering a knifelike chop to the last soldier. The blow was so perfectly executed that its movement seemed effortless and slow. Chiun's hand, extended in a plane from the billowing sleeve of his robe, glided like a piece of metal toward the soldier's throat. When it struck, there was a snap of neck bones and the quick bounce of the man's head. And then, as if the old hands were knives slicing through paper, the head fell cleanly off the body in a spray of blood and rolled down the mountainside. The rest of the body twitched once and then came to rest on a carpet of pine needles.

When it was all over, the old Oriental put his hands back into his sleeves. He kicked the soldier's fallen Uzi and sent it clattering down the rocky slope. A burst of gunfire shattered the silence a moment later.

"Shoddy merchandise," the Korean said.

Remo hunkered down and examined one of the bodies. "Army-issue clothing dyed black," he said. "And they moved like soldiers, too."

"Perhaps your government has changed the color of its military uniforms," Chiun offered. "I never did think they were appropriate. That green," he made a gesture of dismissal, "so close to the hue of monkey excrement. Black is better for warrior's garb."

"Maybe," Remo said, "but I don't think these guys are from any branch of our service. Veterans, maybe. Probably mercs. The leader talked like an American."

Karen stepped up behind Remo and rested her hand on his shoulder. He could feel her shaking.

"Don't look at this," he said. He led her back to the clearing. "Are you all right?"

She nodded. "But I have to go. I've got to get to the police."

"Okay," Remo said. "Sam'll take you in the jeep." He looked around. "Sam?"

"Will somebody get me down?" a quavering voice requested from above. Remo looked up and saw Wolfshy waving at him from the branch of the ponderosa pine where Remo had deposited him.

Remo made a half-turn and a second later Wolfshy felt himself floating to the ground.

"Say, where did you guys learn that stuff? That's some incredible shit."

Chiun glared at him. "It is Sinanju."

"Far, far out," Wolfshy said admiringly. "How long does it take to learn something like that? I've seen those ads in the backs of magazines. You know, the Quick Way to Killing Power . . . Thirty Days to a Better Build, things like that. You just mail in the coupon—''

''It takes a lifetime,'' Remo said.

''Longer, if you're white,'' Chiun added.

''Well, I'm *red*. I bet I could pick that up in a couple of weeks. I was watching. It's all in the wrist, isn't it? If I just—''

''If you just shut up, you can take Karen into Santa Fe,'' Remo said.

''Uh-uh, no way,'' Wolfshy said. ''She'll be safe going down the mountain. You guys might need me.''

''Highly unlikely,'' Chiun said.

''Well, what about just now?''

''Just now with the soldiers?'' Remo asked. ''You were in a tree, remember?''

''I was distracting them. Besides, you hired a guide, right?''

''Yes,'' Chiun said dryly. ''Unfortunately, we got you.''

''Sam's right,'' Karen said. ''There aren't going to be any soldiers between here and the city. But I'll need the jeep.''

''Whoa,'' Wolfshy said. ''Nobody said anything about loaning my jeep. Neither a borrower nor a lender be. Anyway, that northeast trail's going to be rough on the engine.''

Remo sighed. ''The route into Santa Fe runs due south.'' He reached into Wolfshy's jacket, extracted the keys, and tossed them over to Karen. ''I think you'll be better off without him anyway.''

Karen caught the keys and smiled. "One thing," Remo said. "When you get to the police, don't mention us, okay? Just tell them you escaped and then stole the jeep from an empty campsite. Sam can pick it up later."

"Okay." She kissed him softly. "Thanks for everything. Thank you all."

When she was gone, Chiun sat back on the ground, his eyes half-closed. "Now perhaps an old man may sleep."

"I'm with you," Remo said. "I'm beat."

"That is unfortunate. Because someone has to clean up that mess you made."

"*I* made? I didn't guillotine anybody."

"Naturally. Your technique is not adequate for precision work. But even such as you may be useful in your way. Clear away this disgusting refuse. These bodies are a blight on the landscape."

"Who are you, Ranger Rick?"

"And take that talkative person with you. Keep him silent if you can."

Wolfshy followed Remo to the first body, but since the sight of blood made him sick, the Indian was of little use.

"You're really worthless," Remo said as Wolfshy lay quivering on the ground after a bout of retching.

"That's what my uncle says. That's what just about everybody says about me."

"Well, just about everybody's right." He hoisted the body onto his shoulders and lugged it down the slope, where he left it in a shallow arroyo.

If it's not trunks, it's bodies, Remo thought bitterly. It

seemed he spent the better part of his life carrying something heavy from one place to another.

The whir of a helicopter sounded in the distance. Alarmed, he strained through the darkness to make out its lights. The chopper seemed to be making a loop around the side of the mountain, but it wasn't coming as far down as their campsite. He relaxed. *Then it hasn't spotted Karen.* It was probably searching for the band of soldiers that had ambushed them.

The drone receded, grew louder, faded again. *Whoever's running the operation at the top of the mountain*, Remo thought as he lugged the bodies to the arroyo, *he's got his own private army*.

The sound droned on. Remo felt his palms moisten. He didn't like the sound of helicopters. Or gunfire. Or children screaming. They reminded him of the war, and more than all the other hurts of his life, he wanted to forget that one.

But he couldn't. Every time he heard a chopper, he remembered.

CHAPTER SEVEN

Mostly he remembered the bodies.

It happened on some jungle hill on the outskirts of some jungle village in Nam. Remo's platoon had run out of rations and were foraging for food, feasting on exotic plumed birds and prehistoric-looking greens. They'd held the Hill for more than six months. It looked like time to get out.

Again.

Only every time the food ran out, choppers would fly in from Malaya or Sumatra with more. And with the choppers would come a fresh influx of sniper fire on the camp.

It was useless. Remo knew it, and so did everybody else in the outfit. Maybe in the whole army. You can't hold a hill with seventy men when you're surrounded by an inexhaustible supply of enemy firearms.

Still, they held it, for weeks, months. And while the men were being picked off one by one, the choppers kept flying in with more food for the ones who were still alive.

The choppers never brought in replacement troops. The only men that flew into that hellhole were occasional CIA agents, looking for God knew what. They came with their sunglasses and fancy handguns and stayed awhile and didn't talk to anybody. Then the CIA men would leave on the next food chopper.

Sometimes the enlisted men would ask the CIA experts when they were getting off the Hill, but the intelligence men either didn't know or wouldn't talk. They didn't have much to do with the army and didn't interfere.

Even with the bodies.

They were the CO's idea.

They started appearing after the first month on the Hill. The men were washed out by then, filthy and isolated and scared to go to sleep at night. The only thing that sustained them was the type of black humor peculiar to men who faced death too often to take it seriously anymore.

All but the CO. He was a major, and he thrived on the Hill. Every morning he was up before the rest of the platoon, dressed and shaved and whistling. He slept like a rock and woke up ready to kill. The major was at his best during an attack, especially when he could fight hand to hand. More than once, Remo had seen him throw back his head in laughter while he strangled a Viet Cong invader with his bare hands.

As time went by, while the other men were quietly descending to subhuman level, the major only got cleaner and brighter and more eager. He loved the action on the Hill. It sent a shiver down everyone's back when they realized that he was never going to pull them out, and that the reason was because he loved it.

Then the bodies came. One sweltering summer morning Remo and the others got up to find the mutilated bodies of six dead VC strung on a wire on the edge of camp. They were tied by their wrists. Their open eyes and gaping wounds were already black with crawling flies.

"A little reminder to the enemy, boys," the major said with a grin, as his troops stared with astonishment. "We're going to surround the camp with their carcasses. That'll teach 'em to fuck with the U.S. Army." With a brief, confident nod, he strode away, as if he had just presented the men with a gift.

There was a CIA man on the Hill then. He'd come a couple of days before. His name was MacCleary, and he looked different from the other intelligence officers who'd been in camp. For one thing, he wasn't the weasel-thin government-issue spy. MacCleary was big, bordering on fat. For another, he had a hook instead of a right hand. MacCleary looked as if he could get mean if he wanted to, but like the others, he seemed determined to mind his own business. Even when he saw the bodies crucified on the wire that hot August morning, he said nothing.

Later that day, Remo approached him. "Get us out of here," he said quietly. "The CO's nuts."

MacCleary spit on his hook and polished it on his trousers. "I know. I can't." He walked away.

Everyday, more bodies were added while the old ones rotted off the wire. Occasionally, a bird would carry a fallen hand a few yards before dropping it, so that the camp was littered with gray, maggot-ridden hands and fingers.

At first, the only bodies strung up were VC who'd tried an attack on the Hill. But when they shied away, the major would send out expeditions to bring back more. Little by little, the camp was surrounded by a curtain of corpses that melted and rotted in the unrelenting sun. The smell of death was everywhere, and no one got used to it. When the circle of bodies around the Hill was complete, the major ordered a second wire to be put up.

And all the time he smiled and shaved and whistled.

It was another hot, fetid morning when Remo saw the first arrivals on the second wire. And heard them.

They were not dead.

Two Vietnamese civilians were hanging, like the corpses, by their wrists. One was an old man with white hair. He was stripped naked. The other was a boy no more than nine or ten years old. He had a bullet wound in his side. The old man moaned softly. The boy, near death, only opened and closed his mouth in short gasps.

"What do you think, Private?" It was the major, cleaner than Remo had ever seen him.

Without a word, Remo cut down the old man and the boy. He held the boy in his arms. The child didn't weigh fifty pounds.

"These people need a doctor," Remo said.

The major scowled. "Did I hear you call these walking garbage heaps *people*, soldier? Get them back up there before I have you court-martialed."

"They're civilians, sir," Remo said, tasting the bile in his mouth.

"They're scum! You hear me? *Scum*. Like you, Williams. Now, you string those VC up, or a court-martial's going to be too good for you."

A few soldiers had come around to see what was causing the commotion. With them was Conrad MacCleary, the CIA man.

Remo set the boy down. "You go straight to hell," he muttered. "Sir."

In a flash the major's knife was out and slashing toward Remo's throat. Remo turned. The blade sliced across the fleshy part of his back.

The major's face hardened into a terrifying grin. "You're going to be sorry you ever said that, Private." His voice was soft as he backed Remo against the hanging bodies.

"Hold it, Major." It was Conrad MacCleary. His hook was pressed into the soft flesh of the major's throat.

"You've got no jurisdiction here."

"No?" MacCleary said. "What do you call this hook?" He jabbed it deeper into the major's neck.

The military man looked wildly to his troops. "Stop him," he croaked.

None of the soldiers moved.

After a long moment, MacCleary released him. The CIA man went to the two prisoners and looked them over. "The boy's already dead," he said. "The old man won't live out the day. Get your men to find him a place to die in peace."

The major obeyed.

The next day the corpses were taken down.

The day after that, the food chopper arrived. MacCleary radioed a message and waited. By six o'clock that evening, the major received orders of transfer, and the men on the Hill were ordered to evacuate.

"I thought you couldn't do anything," Remo told MacCleary.

The big man shrugged. "What did I do? Sicced the fruitcake on some other outfit. I couldn't get him out. Guys like that are good for wars."

"But you got us out of here."

MacCleary grunted.

"Why?"

"Because I want to see you live through this mess. I've seen you before. I've seen you kill."

It was years before Remo saw Conrad MacCleary again and found out that the man he was working for in the CIA was Harold W. Smith. And that MacCleary had come to the Hill looking for an orphan named Remo Williams, because Smith's computers had pegged him as a possible candidate for the enforcement arm of CURE.

Remo never did find out what happened to the major. The episode on the Hill was one he tried not to think about. But sometimes the major's grinning, frighteningly clean face still haunted him, like the sound of helicopter blades.

Major Deke Bauer. The name was etched into his memory as deeply as the image of bodies hanging on wire.

CHAPTER EIGHT

Deke Bauer had the patience that every good soldier required, but at the moment it was stretched to the limit. The major glanced at the clock on the mantel for the hundredth time that night.

Where in the hell were Brickell and his men? They'd gone down the mountain hours ago. They should have returned by now, bringing along with them the bodies of the three intruders.

The mantel clock chimed midnight. Bauer pushed back his chair, crossed the room to the dying fire, and then turned abruptly around, heading for the door. On his way out he scooped up his Uzi and a pair of infrared nightglasses.

He would check out the situation himself. That was the only way he'd get any sleep.

"I'm going out for a while," the major informed the sentry at the main door. "If Brickell and his team get back before I do, tell Brickell to wait in my office for me. I don't care how late it is."

"Yes, sir," the sentry responded quickly. He would not, he thought silently, want to be in Brickell's size twelves for anything right now. The old man was pissed, and someone, probably Brickell, was going to pay the price. In spite of his heavy field jacket, the sentry felt a sudden chill. The money on this job was tops, and any mercenary in the country would jump at the chance to work here, but Bauer was no one to fuck with.

It was cold and windy on the mountaintop. Wisps of fog eddied and swirled around the tall pines. The major kept to the overgrown path, the same one the monks had hacked out of the mountainside nearly a hundred years before. When they'd first taken over the monastery, Bauer considered clearing away all the underbrush that obscured the trail. But then he'd decided it was best left as they'd found it. The buckbrush and high grass were an effective camouflage. Why let anyone else know there was an easy way up and down the mountain?

He smelled smoke. With his nightglasses, he could make out the embers of a campfire. Three figures were lying near it.

Dead?

He watched for another quarter-hour. One of the figures moved. So the intruders were still alive.

Bauer slipped by the clearing where the fire was and then worked his way up from the downwind side. Two tours of duty in Nam had taught him that it was best to arrive from the direction from which you were least expected.

When he found Brickell and the team, he resolved, he'd teach them a lesson they'd never forget. He'd told them to do the job and come straight back. The order had been clearly understood. There was no damn excuse for not carrying it out to the letter.

Bauer clambered over a boulder and dropped softly down into a shallow arroyo. His boot sank into something firm but yielding. Overhead, the moon shook off a bank of ragged clouds. Now Bauer could see the path clearly. What he'd stepped on was someone's stomach.

"Brickell," he whispered, looking down at the shattered remains of the man's face. It was the team leader. . . . No, goddammit, it was the whole *team*. The broken bodies were stacked in a pile like leftover sandwiches from a party to which no one had come.

The major sank down on the rock. "Jesus," he said in a choked whisper as he spotted something a few yards away. He went over to examine it. It was a severed head wedged between two rocks, its blackening eyes wide and seeming to stare right at him. Bauer snaked his hand between the rocks to dislodge it, but it slipped away from him and rolled down the rocks to rest at Brickell's feet.

What the hell happened here? Bauer recalled hearing a single burst of gunfire about a half-hour after he'd sent the team out. He'd assumed he'd heard the three intruders being finished off. But that wasn't what had happened. He kicked the pile of mangled and twisted bodies and realized with a shudder that his men hadn't been shot. Some kind of *thing* had literally torn them apart.

He immediately ruled out the three civilians. If the team had been shot, he would have considered them, but he damn well knew that no three guys, no matter how good they were, could take out a party of well-armed, combat-trained men.

There was nothing he could do here. He'd send a burial party out tomorrow at daybreak. With his automatic cradled in his arms, Bauer began to work his way slowly and cautiously toward the fire.

After an hour, Bauer slowly lowered the nightglasses. His legs felt cramped from crouching so long in one position. His temples throbbed dully, the headache fueled by the rage that had been steadily building inside him. He didn't understand what was going on, and that was what he hated the most. Two guys and an old gook. How in the world could they possibly have slaughtered eight armed men without even using bullets?

The strangest part of it was that he thought he recognized one of the men. The guy with the high cheekbones and the brown hair. There was something familiar about the set of his head and shoulders, as if Bauer should know him well. Still, he couldn't place the man.

He pushed the annoying thought out of his mind. For over an hour now, his finger had been itching to squeeze the trigger, to finish off the interlopers with a couple of bursts of fire. But if it had been that simple, he reminded himself, that's what Brickell would have done. In wartime, you didn't make major by repeating somebody else's mistakes. Particularly when that somebody else was a dead man.

Bauer moved silently back up the mountain, straying off the path for a while in order to give the campsite the widest possible berth. He needed time to think, to come up with some sort of plan. He knew instinctively that they'd head for the monastery tomorrow, maybe as early as first light. That didn't leave him a lot of time.

Ambush?

No. He'd already lost eight good men. He couldn't afford more casualties. He needed something more subtle, and yet with much greater force. He couldn't take any chances this time. He couldn't make the mistake again of underestimating the enemy.

His mind began to play with an idea, vague at first, then suddenly defined in perfect clarity.

It would work.

There was no way that it couldn't.

Slowly, Bauer's hard-set mouth began to relax. It was the kind of idea that made him smile.

CHAPTER NINE

The first rays of the morning sun burned off the ground fog and took the chill out of the air. Birds darted among the towering pines, swooping down to feast off clusters of chokecherry and buckbrush. There was a light breeze, sweet-scented and cool. All in all, it looked like a perfect morning for a climb.

Chiun was the first to rise. He padded over to the fire, tossed a few sticks on the dying embers, and then waited for the fire to gather strength before heating a pot of water for tea. Some twenty minutes later Remo woke up.

"Sleep well?" he asked as he squatted down beside the Oriental.

"Sleep," Chiun drawled accusingly. "Even the dead could not slumber with all that noise. Ata-tata-tat."

"It was a helicopter," Remo said quietly. "But I don't think it spotted us."

With a series of groans, Sam Wolfshy got up and came to the fire, smacking his lips. "What time is it?" he yawned. He tilted back his straw hat and tucked his hair beneath it. "I know you guys wanted to get an early start," he groaned, "but this is ridiculous." The Indian squatted down beside the fire and poured himself a cup of Chiun's tea. "What is this stuff?" He eyed the steaming, greenish-tinted liquid with obvious distaste.

Chiun slapped the cup out of his hands. "It's not for you," he said peevishly.

"I was only going to borrow some."

"Borrow some cloth and tie it around your mouth. We leave in ten minutes."

"Is he always like this in the morning?" Wolfshy asked when Chiun was out of earshot.

"Only on good days. Usually, he's worse."

They started up the mountainside together, Remo taking the point while Chiun and the Indian trailed behind. Of all the times of day, Remo enjoyed the morning the most. There was something about the air and the sunlight, the quiet tranquility of the world before it was completely awake, before it had a chance to fill up with old scars and new memories. Remo smiled. From down below he could hear Chiun's voice reciting a long poem about a butterfly.

"There's the path," Wolfshy exclaimed, clambering over a boulder. "See where the ground is all grown over with buckbrush?"

Chiun hoisted himself up beside him. "Will miracles never cease," he said. "For once, you are right."

Sam beamed.

Then, as if the sky had been torn open, a thunderous explosion knocked them both to the ground. Above them the mountain rumbled and groaned. A second later, the sun was blocked out as a forty-foot wall of rock and earth hurtled down on them.

The air was filled with choking, blinding dust. The terrible sound was everywhere, a deafening scream as the earth collapsed on the three travelers. Remo struggled to keep his footing, relaxing his body instead of tensing it, as Chiun had taught him. He pushed off, launching himself skyward, fighting his way through the onslaught of rocks and dirt.

For a while, he thought this dark, breath-robbing rain would be endless, but he finally broke free above the swirling dust. He blinked to clear his eyes of debris and hung on to the branches of an uprooted pine. The ominous roar of rocks diminished, but he could still see only a few feet in front of his face.

While he caught his breath, the air began to clear. The devastation caused by the landslide was freakish. It was as if some giant hand had torn a gaping hole in the mountain, scooping up a square quarter-mile of earth and then letting it fall on what was below. The campsite was buried under a hundred-foot mound of ashy dust. Towering pines had splintered like matchsticks, the severed trunks sticking out at bizarre angles. All the familiar landmarks had been obliterated. There was nothing below them but a grayish-brown pile of earth, as silent and dead as the day the world began.

Only one thought came to Remo's mind.

Chiun.

The last time he'd seen the old Oriental and the Indian, they'd been crossing a gully, a long channel that snaked halfway up the mountainside. He knew that the hurtling wall of debris would have filled it in a matter of seconds. Chiun would have had considerably less time to leap free, especially since he was encumbered with Wolfshy.

Remo felt himself sweating. He drew a slow breath to relax, but it wasn't working. He was thinking the unthinkable. . . . That Chiun and Wolfshy hadn't made it to safety. That because of their position, they were buried somewhere below, entombed beneath thousands of pounds of rock and earth.

He started to dig, blindly, aimlessly, in the still-swirling clouds of dust.

"Be still," Chiun hissed. He felt the giant boulder shift lightly where it rested on his outstretched fingertips. He could see nothing in the total darkness. He could hear nothing from above. The only sounds were his own carefully measured breathing and the panting and squirming of the Indian beneath him in the small pocket of space they occupied.

"Cease all movement," Chiun whispered in warning. His words were barely audible, but their tone halted Wolfshy's thrashing. "Good. I did not wish to kill you. Imagine the embarrassment if I myself did not survive."

The very thought of it made Chiun wince. Not death; that was merely the gateway to paradise. But to share a grave with a common red-skinned white man of dubious intelligence? Would he drag Chiun along to meet his ancestors? Such a thing would be horrendous.

Therefore, Chiun concluded, he would not die.

It was all the Indian's fault to begin with. Chiun could have carried them both clear if this cretin hadn't insisted on running in the wrong direction. So Chiun had lost the fraction of a second needed to transport them safely above the falling rocks. The old man could have saved himself. After all, he told himself, what was this trembling moron beneath him in comparison with a Master of Sinanju? But the moment had decreed it otherwise. And now Chiun knew that he had to live or die by that decree.

"What's happening?" the Indian whispered.

"Nothing is happening!" Chiun hissed. "When it does, you will surely know. Either the rocks will crush us, or we will be saved. There is little likelihood of any other alternative."

"How come we're not already dead?"

Chiun sighed. Maybe he ought to kill this idiot, after all. Who could blame him? "Because," he explained patiently, "I am holding aloft the rocks that threaten to flatten us. If this were not so, then I would not be able to answer all these stupid questions."

"Sorry," Wolfshy mumbled. "Just curious."

Chiun felt the awesome weight of his burden shift again slightly. Remo, he sensed, must be somewhere above. If the rocks were moved properly, then all would go well. On the other hand, if they were displaced incorrectly, there would be nothing that Chiun could do to save himself or the Indian. Black earth and rock would take the place of the air they breathed, gradually pushing their way into their mouths and nostrils. Even under those conditions Chiun would be able to stave off death for a few hours, but the Indian would be sent into the Void in a matter of seconds. All because the rocks had been moved one way instead of another.

Chiun felt himself at one with the boulder in his hand. Would Remo be equal to the task? he wondered. He had taught the boy well. In spite of his pale skin, there had never been another, even a Korean, who had so quickly learned and mastered the ways of Sinanju. But as Chiun knew all too well, this learning was a process that would never be complete. Remo would go on learning all the years of his life, with perfection, the unattainable goal, always just out of reach. It was meant to be so. Otherwise, Sinanju would not be Sinanju.

The old Oriental heard Remo's voice above him. "Chiun!" it called. "Can you hear me?" It sounded like little more than a whisper in the breeze.

"Of course I can hear you," Chiun said softly. "Stop that caterwauling and get us out of this place."

Above him, he felt rocks shifting purposefully. Remo was working well.

The boulder in the old man's hand began to tremble. A thin trickle of dust swirled in the air. He could feel the gritty particles against his parchmentlike cheek.

"Fast but slow," Chiun murmured to himself. Every breath and heartbeat must be properly executed. A handful of earth misplaced and the darkness would close in on

114

them. But Remo would not fail. Chiun knew that, and the knowledge made the weight of the boulder lighter.

"How'd Remo find us?" Wolfshy asked softly.

"Because he is Remo," Chiun said.

The Indian sat silently for a long time. Finally he said, "It must be a good feeling to know there's someone you can always count on."

"That is what a son is, young man." Chiun's voice was gentle.

Son. That was the way it would always be.

"Son," the old man whispered to himself. Some words, he knew, were destined to be felt and yet never uttered.

CHAPTER TEN

Miles Quantril sat in the passenger seat of the helicopter as it passed over the southern slope of the mountain. "Turn around," he ordered the pilot. "And get down closer."

Beside him, the pilot nodded as he eased the chopper around in a low, swooping circle around the desolate wreckage of the slope. His hands trembled slightly as he maneuvered the controls. Flying Mr. Quantril always made him nervous.

"What the hell happened down there?" Quantril's face was pressed against the Plexiglas bubble as if he intended to gnaw his way through it.

"Looks like a landslide, sir," the pilot said.

"I can see that, you ass. How did it happen? Why?"

The pilot chewed on his lower lip. "I don't know, sir."

Quantril felt a rage building inside him as he took in the gigantic spill of rock and earth, with its twisted and broken trees and huge boulders jutting out unnaturally. It was a surprise, and Quantril hated surprises. Anything that he didn't plan himself, he believed, ought not to happen. When it did happen, the feeling of his own helplessness infuriated him. "Take me to the monastery."

"Yes, sir," the pilot answered quickly. Once they landed, Mr. Quantril would let out his anger on someone else.

The chopper landed on the monastery roof. The pilot cut the engine, but Quantril made no move to disembark. He was staring straight ahead, his manicured hands idly toying with a slender gold fountain pen.

"We're here, sir," the pilot reminded him.

Miles Quantril turned toward the pilot. "That fact has not escaped me," he said testily. He tapped the pen against his knee. "Do you know how I feel when I'm faced with a flagrant deviation from a carefully laid plan?"

The pilot swallowed. "No, sir," he said, suddenly feeling trapped.

"I feel like killing someone. It doesn't particularly matter who. It's the act itself that ventilates my anger. I believe in ventilating. Don't you?"

The pilot wiped a line of perspiration off his forehead. "Mr. Quantril, I'm a family man," he said. "I've got a wife and four kids."

"Why should I care about your family?"

The pilot was silent.

Quantril spoke softly. "Frankly, I can't think of one reason not to kill you in thirty seconds. Can you?" He smiled.

He was kidding. He had to be kidding, the pilot told

himself. Still, he could not control the fluttering of his hands. The vinyl seat beneath him was damp and sticky with sweat. His throat seemed to be made of ash. ''That's— that's very funny, sir,'' he said, forcing a wan smile.

Quantril reached into his white linen jacket and produced a revolver made of chrome and mother-of-pearl. ''Twenty seconds,'' he said, smiling back at the man.

''But I'm a pilot. That's it, I'm a pilot. If you kill me, there won't be anyone else to fly you back to Santa Fe.''

The next few seconds were the longest in the pilot's life.

''Very good,'' Quantril said finally. ''You came up with a reason. You didn't buckle under pressure. You're a good soldier.''

The pilot closed his eyes with relief.

''Unfortunately for you, however,'' Quantril said, cocking the gun, ''I'm a licensed pilot myself. Helicopters and light planes. Your time is up.'' He fired.

The door opened and the pilot's body spilled out onto the roof. A moment later, Quantril stepped jauntily over the body toward the waiting line of men standing at attention.

Deke Bauer saluted him, ignoring the pilot's bloody body.

''What's the meaning of the landslide down there?''

''It was an avalanche, sir,'' Bauer said. ''A planned avalanche.''

''Really.'' Quantril was interested. ''I dabble in explosives myself. Let's hear about it.''

Bauer explained about the three men who were sighted coming up the mountain after the girl escaped. He told Quantril about sending out the raiding party and how he himself had discovered their remains. He described the white man, the Indian, and the Oriental in detail. Then he began to smile as he related how he had planted the explosives that triggered the landslide. He was actually grinning when he got to the explosion itself and the rain of destruction it unleashed on the civilians who had dared to trespass on the mountain.

"All that for just three people?" Quantril demanded.

"Yes, sir," Bauer said. "If you'd seen what my men looked like, you would have done the same thing, sir. There was a massacre down there."

Quantril's eyes narrowed. "What kind of weapons did they use?"

"That's the weird part," Bauer said. "There wasn't any shooting."

Quantril sucked in his breath. "Who were they?"

"Unknown, sir. But I've dispatched a team to recover the bodies of the intruders." His lips twitched at the thought.

"What about the girl? Was she with them?"

"No. She probably didn't reach them at the time of the avalanche. She was traveling on foot. But she's dead now."

"Good," Quantril said. "How'd she get out in the first place? I thought the security in this place was tight."

"It is, sir. She was just lucky. For a while. Some Mexie here helped her escape. I'm taking care of her now."

Quantril looked up in alarm. "You're not—"

"I'm not hitting their faces."

Quantril's mouth formed a slow smile. "But you'd like to, wouldn't you, Deke?"

Bauer grinned. The boss was okay. Quantril was a little slick, maybe, but underneath they were two of a kind. "Maybe a little," he confessed, and the two men laughed.

Quantril put his arm around Bauer's shoulders. "Oh, Deke," he whispered, "I'd like to look over the stock, if you know what I mean."

"I think I know," Bauer said.

"After all, I can't give away gifts without seeing the merchandise first, can I?"

"No, sir."

Quantril's gaze swept over the roof. "How about a little dress parade, Deke? Here on the roof."

"Right away, sir."

"Without dress." He winked. "Got me?"

"Gotcha, sir." The major raced down the stone steps toward the prison.

They appeared in single file, like a vision in a dream: 180 beautiful young women, stark naked, their bodies ripe and inviting as they were marched past the rows of armed guards.

Quantril looked them over carefully as he passed down the line, brushing his hands against their soft breasts and bellies.

"A little soiled, but acceptable," he said approvingly.

"They've had the best of care, sir," Bauer assured him.

Quantril stopped in front of Consuela Madera. "This one is especially nice." He fondled the mass of black curls on her head. "Yes, especially. I may keep her for myself."

Consuela stiffened. "What have you done with Karen?" she demanded.

"Who?"

Deke Bauer answered. "Karen Lockwood. The blonde that got out. This is the Mexie bitch that helped her."

Quantril's eyebrows rose. "And she went unpunished?"

"Body blows, sir." Bauer chuckled.

Quantril saw the bruises on Consuela's abdomen and traced them with his finger. "Ah, yes. Good work, Bauer." He felt himself being aroused. "I'm glad you didn't touch her face. I so despise ugly women."

"What did you do with her?" Consuela shrilled.

Quantril yanked her hair, snapping her head backward. "You speak when you're spoken to like a good girl, understand? Or should I teach you some manners?" He jerked her head back farther. Her defiant eyes welled with tears of pain. The sight made Quantril's erection throb. He moved close to the woman. "Your friend is dead," he whispered. "And you're mine."

Consuela spat in his face.

With a howl of disgust, Quantril pulled back his arm and cannoned it across the woman's mouth. She fell backward, her back scraping against the broken tile of the roof.

"Slimy foreign bitch." He pulled out his chrome-plated revolver, then yanked her by her hair to her feet. "Let's see what your face looks like after this." He cocked the weapon and held it dead center against her eye.

She trembled with fear. The smell of her excited him. "On second thought," he said, "I think another way may be even more interesting. Bauer!"

"Sir?"

"Escort the lady to the wall."

Bauer led Consuela to the notched wall that surrounded the roof. With the butt of his Uzi, he forced the naked woman to step into the space between the battlements.

Below was a sheer drop of 1,500 feet into the valley. The wind whistled forbiddingly through Consuela's hair. She shivered as Quantril approached her from behind. "You're going to jump, *muchacha*," he teased. "By the time we're through with you, you're going to want to jump."

He turned back to Bauer. "Have your men bring up some stones."

"Stones, sir?"

"About the size of baseballs, maybe smaller. Nice round throwing stones."

Bauer's face broke into an expectant grin. "Yes, sir." The major sent off a half-dozen men, including Corporal Kains, the women's guard. While the other men scurried to the stairwell, Kains stood rigid, his eyes on the floor.

"You waiting for a personal invitation, Corporal?" Bauer boomed.

Kains blinked rapidly. "It's not right, sir," he said quietly. "He wants to stone her."

Bauer bristled. "*He* is Mr. Quantril, and whatever Mr. Quantril wants, Mr. Quantril gets, understand?"

"Not from me, sir," Kains said, his beast's eyes looking frightened but stubborn.

Quantril came over.

"I'll straighten him out, sir," Bauer began.

Quantril waved him away. "It's all right. Your man just has principles. Isn't that right, soldier?"

Kains was sweating profusely. "I don't know, sir. I only know I'm not going to help torture Consuela."

"So it's Consuela, is it? Maybe she's something special to you?"

Kains flushed.

"Well, well. I think we've got a real loverboy here, Bauer. What do you think?"

"He's been trouble from the beginning, sir. It was Kains who let the Lockwood girl escape."

"Well, well," Quantril repeated. He walked over to the parapet where Consuela was standing and looked over. "It's a long way down there," he said. "Maybe Corporal Kains would like to show his lady love what the trip's going to be like."

Kains's face turned white.

"Let's have an escort for the corporal, Bauer," Quantril said.

Bauer barked an order. Four men with the expressionless faces of born thugs stepped forward to grasp Kains's arms. The soldier's feet skidded as he tried to stop the momentum of the men leading him to the wall. When they reached the parapet, Kains looked up at the horrified woman standing on the brink, and his eyes filled with sudden tears.

"Don't be afraid, Consuela," he shouted hoarsely, scrabbling at the wall with bleeding fingers. Then the soldiers forced him through and he fell, his arms windmilling, his hair blowing wildly in the wind.

He never screamed.

Consuela turned away, sobbing. There was a scramble of footsteps on the stairs. Five soldiers appeared, holding helmets filled with stones.

"That was just the opening act," Quantril said with a ringmaster's flourish. He picked up one of the stones and hefted it. "And now, ladies and gentlemen, the feature attraction."

He took aim and threw the rock. It struck Consuela on the back of one knee, causing her legs to buckle. The other women hushed as she teetered on the edge of the parapet trying to regain her balance. As soon as she did, Quantril threw another rock that hit her square in the middle of her back.

"Be my guest, fellows," he invited. The four soldiers and Bauer helped themselves to stones from their helmets. Bauer yelped in triumph as one of his stones rapped the girl on the back of her head, producing a spurt of blood.

Consuela bent over pitifully, her limbs shaking as the blows dug into her flesh.

None of the other women dared speak. The only sounds were the raucous shouts of the six men hurling rocks as if at some inanimate target, and the dull thumps as they hit the woman's battered body.

"Aren't you ever going to jump, bitch?" Bauer shouted gleefully. "Maybe we should've washed her up first. Them Mexies are so dirty, their feet stick to anything."

The men howled with laughter. Bauer drew back,

taking aim again, when he saw a sentry rushing over to him.

"You want some action, too?" the major said, his eyes feverish with excitement. "Here, see what you can do."

"Sentry report, sir," the young soldier said. "There are three men approaching the mission. Civilians, sir."

Bauer felt something tighten inside him. "What'd they look like?" he asked warily.

The soldier thought. "One of 'em's white, tall, skinny. One's an Indian or something. Long black hair. The third one's an old gook, maybe a hundred years old. Looks like he'd keel over if you breathed on him too hard."

Quantril dropped the stone he was holding. "Weren't they the men you blew up the mountain for?"

Bauer's face twisted. "It can't be them, sir. They've got to be dead." He looked into the valley. "They've got to be."

CHAPTER ELEVEN

"You're really something," Sam Wolfshy said for the hundredth time as they neared the peak of the mountain.

Since their escape from being buried alive, Chiun had become even more of a hero to the Indian than he had been before. "I can't get over it," Wolfshy said. "That Sinanju stuff is the greatest. You got to teach it to me, Chiun, okay?"

"Do not insult the sun source of the martial arts by associating yourself with it," the old man said crankily.

The Indian was undaunted. "If you'll give me lessons, I'll pay you for them later," he said. "It'll be sort of like borrowing a little information."

"The art of Sinanju requires more than a little information, O lard brain," Chiun said. He cocked his head. "Although you are correct. I was quite remarkable. To hold up the boulder as I did is a feat of extraordinary discipline, both mental and physical. Without my perfect breathing and impeccable timing, we would never have escaped from the bowels of the earth alive." He polished his fingernails on the sleeve of his robe.

"Hey, wait a minute. I'm the one that got you out," Remo groused.

"Oh, yes," Chiun conceded. "You performed quite adequately—for a white thing."

"For a—"

"Look at my robe. It is in tatters. Remo, remind me to get some others on our next trip to Sinanju."

"You mean there really is such a place?" Wolfshy asked. "Can I go?"

"Certainly not," Chiun said. "I would be laughed out of my village if I were to take you. Besides, you would manage to get us lost on the way."

For the first time, the Indian showed dismay. "I found the path, didn't I?" His head hung low.

"Cheer up, Sam," Remo said. "Sinanju isn't exactly the garden spot of the world."

"But I want to see it. I want to learn what you guys do. I know—"

"Hold it. Look over that rise."

Over a grass-covered knoll rose the bell tower of the monastery. In the center of the crumbling outer wall were twin gates of rough-hewn timber bound together by thick bands of iron. Even though the place had housed an order of holy men, it looked like a fort. The analogy became even more pronounced as the three men watched a dozen black-clad soldiers spread along the top of the wall.

Their gun barrels caught and reflected the late-morning sunlight.

And there was something else up there, too. Remo squinted to look into the light. "I think there's a woman standing on the wall."

The small nude figure crouched, holding onto her elbows.

"Huh? Where?" Wolfshy asked, straining unsuccessfully to see.

"She has been beaten," Chiun observed. "This must be the place you seek."

From the deep grass on the valley floor came a low groan.

"Try to get into the monastery," Remo told Chiun. "Sam, you take cover. I think we've been spotted."

He waded into the deep grass, searching for the source of the sound. He almost gasped when he saw Kains, or what was left of him. His arms and legs lay immobile in unnatural positions. Bones in his chest and arms jutted brokenly through his black uniform. Kains coughed, and a fountain of blood spurted from his lips.

"Jesus," Remo whispered.

"Forgive me, Father, for I have sinned." The words came out in a feeble whisper.

Remo tried to dredge in the faraway corners of his memory for some words of comfort. He had been raised as a Catholic in the orphanage, but he could remember nothing that would make death easier for this or any other man.

"He forgives you," Remo said. He was not a religious man, but he couldn't believe that God could look at a man as mangled as Kains and turn His back on him.

129

"Thank you," Kains mumbled. Blood oozed out of the corner of his mouth. "I did it for Consuela."

"Sure, kid," Remo said. He arranged the young soldier's limbs into a more normal appearance.

"But Quantril's going to kill her all the same."

Remo's ears prickled at the name. It was too uncommon and too famous. "Who's Quantril?"

Kains's lips quivered in an effort to speak. "Quantril's the boss. Rich man."

"Miles Quantril? The big business type?"

"He's a killer, mister. You got to stop him. Oh, Consuela. . . ."

"Take it easy," Remo said.

"She was so pretty."

"Yeah. Try not to talk."

"It was all I could do."

Remo looked over the dying man. "It was enough," he said. "You kept her alive."

Kains smiled once, as if he were watching something far away. Then a low, gurgling sound bubbled up out of his throat. The soldier tensed in one weak spasm and then died. Remo closed the man's eyes.

Before he could rise, a grenade exploding at his feet knocked him over in a violent somersault.

He dived for cover in a grove of piñon trees. A bullet cracked the air and kicked up a cloud of dust near his face. Five more shots were fired in rapid sequence, splintering a large tree nearby. On the monastery wall, the lone naked woman was replaced by a swarm of men in black moving like spiders along the fortification's outer edge.

Ducking the gunfire, Remo peered out to spot Chiun. The old Oriental was near the front gates of the monastery, walking forward with great dignity and ceremony. Behind him Wolfshy slinked, crouching in the shadow of Chiun's tiny frame.

He's drawing the fire away from me, Remo thought. It was the right thing to do. Remo needed a clear path.

Like dying crows, a rain of black hand grenades fell from the monastery wall onto Chiun and the Indian. Effortlessly, Chiun snapped them out of the air as quickly as they fell and lobbed them back to the other side with a flick of his finger.

It was Remo's cue. He aimed himself for the wall and barreled for it at full speed. As he neared the fortress, he felt the force of gravity pulling at his cheeks and lips.

Above him on the roof of the building could be heard the sound of women screaming. But they were screams of fear, not of pain, and the voices came from the opposite side of the roof from where Chiun had returned the grenades.

The old man had taken it all into consideration, Remo thought. By the time Remo reached the wall, he was almost flying. His legs kept moving at exactly the same pace as he ran out of ground and into a vertical stone wall, but because of his momentum, there was no difference in his stride.

Remo could climb walls from a dead halt, but it required delicate balance, and the act could only be performed slowly, by easing his feet and fingers along the surface. Moving so slowly, he would have made too easy a target. The way he scaled it now, the soldiers standing

131

on the edge of the parapets saw little more than a blur as
Remo vaulted over the top. Even before he landed, he was
slashing with both hands, feeling two necks unjoint under
his knuckles.

Remo did not need to see. From the moment he started
his run in the valley, all of his normal sensations were
blocked out, replaced by a feeling of occupied space. He
himself was an object in that space, and so were the
soldiers around him. They were all units of weight, and
Remo could feel that weight as it shifted and turned around
him. He kicked out behind him, not because he heard the
soldier's stealthy tread or the whoosh of the weapon as it
scraped softly against the man's uniform to rest in firing
position, but because Remo felt the space behind him as
the soldier occupied it. His foot struck the soldier in the
abdomen. From the muted crack of vertebrae, which Remo
felt on the sole of his foot, he knew the soldier's back was
broken.

Effortlessly, without thought, he raised his elbow in a
lightning-quick movement. It caught another black-garbed
soldier in the jaw, spinning the man's head around with a
sharp crack. Remo's arms moved continuously. As the
space around him began to open up, he heard the throaty
gurgles of the dying and the rapid tattoo of a man's boots
on the tile roof of the monastery as he convulsed with his
last breath.

Then the gunfire began. He had only, he realized, gone
through the first line of defense. Forcing his eyes to work,
he now saw a group of soldiers, armed with submachine
weapons, lined along the wall on three sides. On the

fourth side, behind Remo, huddled the screaming, naked women.

He could not let the soldiers fire on him. He himself could dodge the bullets if he had to, but the women could not.

The leader of the armed soldiers advanced, and the men along all three walls edged in closer toward Remo.

"Aim," the leader commanded.

The soldiers moved forward another step.

Then Remo saw it: a scrap of blue brocade billowing behind the moving line of guards; and he knew he was unstoppable now.

He raised himself off the ground in a jump so well-controlled that he seemed to be levitating; then he began his descent. He glided down in a flying wedge, his feet landing firmly on the chest of the lead attacker. The soldier screamed, his Uzi spiraling out of his hands. The force of the blow sent him flying toward the wall, where he caromed off the top edge, spun in midair as if by magic, and then hurtled head first into the valley below.

The others, surprised by the strange trajectory of their leader's path, hesitated a moment before firing.

A moment was enough. Chiun whirled through the formal ranks of soldiers in a neat inside line attack, killing each man in turn as he wove between them. The old man moved so fast that not even Remo could follow the motions of his hands and feet. But he knew that each blow was perfect from the crisp, rhythmic, deadly sounds of impact.

While Chiun worked, Remo gathered the women together and moved them as unobtrusively as possible toward the stairwell. One of them was so covered with lacerations and bruises that she could not walk. Her long dark hair was matted with blood. Her face was gashed and swollen, but despite her wounds, Remo could tell that she was a great beauty.

"Are you Consuela?" Remo asked, picking her up gently.

The woman nodded, trying to force open her bruised eyes.

"There's a dead man in the valley who loved you," he said. Then he stopped short.

He heard a sound from the other side of the bell tower, a sound that to him was as unmistakable as a baby's cry or the crack of gunfire: it was the sound of a helicopter.

Forgetting he still held the woman in his arms, he walked a few paces to see beyond the tower. The chopper was a large Grumman painted bright blue, and two men were getting inside. The first was dressed in stylish civilian clothes, the other in the all-black fatigues of the soldiers who'd defended the monastery. The civilian crawled into the helicopter without a backward look. The other glanced behind him briefly, turned away, then froze where he stood and turned again. He had recognized Remo.

And Remo remembered the soldier's face, too. It was a face of death and torture, of severed hands and dying children. For Remo, Major Deke Bauer possessed the face of war.

Remo's mind was suddenly a confusion of banished images and sensations: a skewered bird, roasted, its white plumes blowing in the breeze before a jungle downpour; a line of bodies suspended on wire, seeming to dance an eerie jig by morning's first light; the stench of rotting flesh.

A low groan escaped from his lips. The superhuman reflexes drilled into him through a decade of Chiun's teaching vanished. For him, now, there was no Sinanju. There was nothing but the war and the endless, futile comedy of the Hill.

As if it were occurring in slow motion, he watched Bauer snap his Uzi into position.

"A chopper'll be coming tomorrow with rations. . . ." said a faraway voice in his memory.

"I took the Hill, and I'm going to keep the Hill, and I don't care if every last one of you bastards dies for it. . . ."

"Put up a second wire. That'll teach 'em not to fuck with the U.S. Army. . . ."

"Get down!" The voice, panicky and loud, startled Remo as he fell to the ground with the woman, screaming, in his arms. Sam Wolfshy's arms were still outstretched. And then he heard the bullets, and the Indian collapsed on top of Remo and the woman in a spray of blood.

"Oh, my God," Remo said, coming to his senses. "Sam!"

The chopper's whirling blades beat the air. It lifted off gracefully, hovered for a moment, and then sped off toward the horizon.

Chiun finished off the last soldier in his attack and came to them. With deft hands he lifted the big Indian off Remo and Consuela.

Sam's arm had been all but blown off at the shoulder. The old Oriental made a quick tourniquet from a length of silk torn from his robe. "He will live," he said. "For a while. How long I cannot say. But he cannot make the descent down the mountain, even if we carry him."

Remo remained where he had fallen, his face dazed. Vaguely he felt the woman slipping from his arms. "He saved us," Consuela said. "Otherwise, the bullets . . ."

"Yes, I saw," Chiun said. He looked down at the Indian. "I knew he had something of the hero in him," he said softly.

Wolfshy's lips curved into a smile. His eyes opened slowly. "I heard that," he whispered. "Think you can teach me Sinanju now?"

Chiun placed his cool hand on Sam's brow. "My son, courage such as yours is beyond any discipline."

Remo turned away. He had seen a man's face, and that look had probably cost Sam Wolfshy's life. It was the one unpardonable sin, and Remo had committed it. He had forgotten Sinanju.

It was the chopper, he said to himself. *The damned chopper. . . .*

And suddenly he could hear it again, menacing and inexorable, the helicopter in his mind that would lead him to madness.

But it wasn't in his mind. Consuela burst into a flurry of Spanish as she pointed to the eastern horizon.

Remo saw it, too. It was coming from the opposite direction from where Bauer's helicopter had gone. As it drew nearer, he could see that its markings were different, too. It was a police helicopter.

"Karen!" Consuela gasped. "She must have contacted the police before she died."

Chiun smiled. "Our yellow-haired friend is with them."

"How can you see that far?" The Mexican woman looked at him, bewildered.

"Don't ask," Wolfshy said.

The Korean was on his feet. "We must be quick. The police will find you medicine and a place to rest, son. But you must not mention that Remo and I were with you."

"Why not? You did—"

"It is our Emperor's wish that we remain anonymous. Tell the authorities that you acted alone." He took a final look at Consuela. "And tell these women to clothe themselves. It is disgraceful."

He lifted Remo up by the ribs and propelled him toward the stairwell. By the time the police helicopter landed and Karen Lockwood and the officers got out, the two of them were deep in the valley, out of sight.

CHAPTER TWELVE

By nightfall, Remo and Chiun were near the foothills of the mountain range. Remo had not spoken since Deke Bauer's bullets tore across the sunlit monastery roof. Those bullets had almost killed Sam Wolfshy, and it had been Remo's fault.

How could I forget? Remo asked himself again and again. How could I ignore all the discipline and training of Sinanju because of a moment's memory?

The sight of Deke Bauer's face had caused him to lose control. But he had let it happen. At the moment when he most needed his skills and confidence, he had lost them. And Sam Wolfshy had paid the price for Remo's failure.

At the edge of a barren copse, near a streambed trickling with water, Chiun finally let go of his pupil's arm and told him to sit down. Remo obeyed, his face a tense mask of self-hatred.

Chiun built a fire. Then, with a stone, he fashioned a bowl from a piece of wood and filled it with water. He untied a small silk pouch from the belt of his robe, poured its contents into the water-filled bowl, then set the bowl on the fire.

"It is rice," he said softly. "Even Masters of Sinanju must eat."

Remo stood up and turned away.

"And so must you, whether you feel you deserve it or not," the old man added pointedly.

Remo leaned against a tree. He remained there, his eyes focused inward, until the rice was cooked. Finally he walked over and knelt beside the old man. "I want you to do me a favor," he said, so quietly that he was almost inaudible.

"So the white man speaks at last. Of course, his first words are to demand some service of me. But I am prepared. Go ahead."

"I want you to go back to Smitty and tell him I'm through."

The expression on Chiun's face did not change. "Because you failed?"

Remo hung his head. "Yeah." A puff of mirthless laughter came from his lips. "Just a little. Sam only got his arm blown off because of me."

Chiun helped himself to the rice. "Well," he said, "for once I agree with you. You have failed miserably."

Remo expected him to say more, but when the old man only went on with his meal in silence, Remo stood up. "That's that, then. I guess I'll leave you here."

Chiun nodded. "Yes, yes. But before you go, Remo, let me ask you one question. Have you never failed before?"

"Not like this."

"Ah." He chewed another mouthful of rice.

After what seemed like an eternity, Remo said, "What does that mean? 'Ah'?"

"Nothing. Only that a great lesson has been shown to you. But evidently you have chosen not to learn from it."

"What are you talking about?" Remo shouted. The veins in his neck stood out. "I'm walking away from everything that means anything to me."

"Why?"

"Because I don't deserve it, damn it!"

"Ah," Chiun repeated. "As I thought."

Remo took a deep breath. "I suppose you knew I was going to quit."

"Of course."

"Oh, excuse me," Remo said nastily. "I underestimated your powers as a prophet."

"Not as a prophet. As a historian."

"This never happened before."

"Not to you," Chiun said. "But to another. Shall I tell you the story, or are you eager to dart aimlessly into the darkness?"

Remo shot him a disgusted look, then sat down. "This better not be about how the Masters of Sinanju had to hire themselves out as assassins to feed their starving villagers."

"It is," Chiun said cheerfully.

Remo rolled his eyes. But it would be the last time, he thought. Even if it was a story he'd heard Chiun tell countless times before, he wanted to hear it again. "Okay," he said.

"I have never before told you the full story of the Great Wang, first real Master of Sinanju," Chiun began. "You know only that he was the one to save his village by offering his services as an assassin to foreign monarchs. But you do not know how Wang came upon the idea. You see, it was the Master himself who brought on the misfortune that destroyed his village and made his people starve."

"Wang? I thought he was the Dudley Do-Right of the East."

"Then listen, my son." The old man settled his robe around him. Lit by moonlight, his parchmentlike skin seemed to glow as he told the ancient legend.

"Wang did not become Master until well into his fifth decade," Chiun said. "But he was a hero among his people from the time he was a young man. As a youth, he used the discipline of Sinanju, which he himself developed, to protect the village from the invading soldiers of a greedy prince. The villagers loved him for his deeds of valor. They draped his house with garlands and showered honors upon him. He was known to them all as Wang the Invincible.

"A yearly festival was set up in his honor. During the proceedings, all the young men of the village would pit their strength and cunning against the mighty Wang. They could not defeat him, of course, because even in those days the the talents of the House of Sinanju were incomparable. But Wang pretended to struggle with the competitors, and each one came away with a feeling of accomplishment.

"The villagers who did not compete sold trinkets and made music and danced and feasted, and the celebration of Wang the Invincible was a day of gaiety and cheer for all.

"But during one festival—the last—a small child wandered away from the village toward the seashore. It was a windy day, and the sea was turbulent, tossing many beautiful shells onto the seaweed-strewn rocks of the coast. The child saw the shells and, since he was alone, climbed down the rocks to play with them. But the rocks were slippery, and the ocean wild. The child was drowned.

"When Wang heard of the tragedy, he visited the child's grieving parents. They had dressed the drowned boy in his best clothes and laid him out before burial. It was there that Wang noticed that the boy's fingers had been scraped nearly to the bone. He realized that the boy had not been drowned quickly, but had clung to life until his last breath on some cold piece of rock. And he knew also that the boy had called for help for all the terrible hours that he held onto the rock, but no one could hear him above the music and laughter of the festival. You see, no one was listening—not even Wang, whose duty it was to protect the people of his village."

"But—but it wasn't his fault," Remo said.

"No? For the pleasure of an afternoon, Wang had permitted a life to be sent into the Void unnecessarily. Was he not to blame?"

Remo was quiet for some moments. "What did he do?" he asked at last.

"What you have planned," Chiun said. "As penance for his negligence, he took himself to the caves of Sinanju, where he lived in solitude for thirty years without even the sound of another voice to comfort him."

Remo nodded. It was a stiff sentence, but he could see the justice of it.

"During that time, invading armies tore the village of Sinanju to pieces, until there were no crops, no trades—not even fish in the sea. The conquering prince knew that without Wang the villagers would offer no resistance, and so he took what he wanted from Sinanju and then left it to die. The villagers grew so poor that they had to send their infant children back to the sea because there was no food for them.

"Then, in his fifty-seventh year, Wang returned to Sinanju. Seeing the ruins of his village, he realized that the thirty years he had spent atoning for his sin had been wasted. For in those thirty years, the drowned boy had not returned to life, and Wang had not been present to fight for his village either.

"He went to the ocean in anguish, and asked of the God of the Sea, 'Why was it ordained thus? The sacrifice of three decades of my life was for nothing. It has brought only more failure and more shame to my heart.'

"The sea rumbled. The sky darkened. At last the voice of the God of the Sea boomed out like a thunderclap: 'Has it brought enough, then?' And at last Wang understood that sometimes the only way to learn is to fail.

"On that day did Wang go forth to distant lands, trading his skills in exchange for gold to feed the starving people of Sinanju. To accomplish this, he had to set aside his shame over the past for the sake of the future. For he realized that although he was not a perfect man, he would do his best and never look back. It was then and only then that Wang became Master. He was the first, and the greatest of us all. Do you not think, my son, that Wang's failure was as much a part of him as his successes?''

Remo nodded slowly. ''Thank you, Little Father,'' he whispered.

''Have some rice. But don't eat it all.''

CHAPTER THIRTEEN

Early evening was Al Meecher's favorite time of day.
Especially the half-hour between six and six-thirty. His
dinner was over and the dishes were stacked and dried.
That was when he poured himself a second cup of coffee
from the pot on the stove and took it into the living room,
where he could read the evening paper, sip his coffee, and
relax. For a short time, he could forget about his failing
business, his ex-wife and her shark lawyer, and the ever-
increasing stack of bills on the hall table.

Meecher's wife had left him a year before, taking every
cent in the savings and joint checking accounts. She'd also
taken the family dog, a cocker spaniel named Bingo. It
had only taken a few weeks for Meecher to realize that he
missed the dog a hell of a lot more than he did his wife.
The dog had been loyal, cheerful, and obedient—everything
Ethel hadn't been.

Meecher settled into the padded armchair and took a sip of coffee. Maybe, he thought, opening his paper, he ought to get another dog. He certainly couldn't afford another wife. But a dog would be nice. He let the idea roam free in his mind for a few seconds. It was just the kind of undemanding companionship he needed. Someone to share this big, empty apartment with. Someone who'd sit with him on the balcony and watch the world go by. The only view the balcony offered was of the monolithic Dream Date building across the street, but for Meecher and his dog, it would be enough.

Now that the idea had taken hold, Meecher knew it was right. Ethel and the shark lawyer would probably bleed him dry, but they wouldn't get his dog, not this time. He was so pleased at the prospect of a new Bingo that he put down the paper, unread for the first time in years. He padded into the bedroom, slipped on a sports coat, and picked up his wallet from the dresser. The pet store on Sunrise Avenue was still open.

Meecher felt a growing sense of excitement. Maybe this was what he'd needed all along, another purpose to his life, no matter how small it might be. This just might be a turning point, he decided. Maybe a dog would help turn his life around. He whistled cheerfully as he headed for the door. His plump hand was on the knob when the doorbell rang. Probably Morty from down the hall, he thought. He'd invite Mort along. Morty would get a real kick out of helping Meecher choose Bingo II.

Smiling, Meecher opened the door. There was a soft, popping sound as a single bullet from the silenced Colt pierced his heart. He sagged to his knees and then toppled over, hitting the carpeted foyer with a gentle thud.

"Let's get him inside," Bauer said. "We wouldn't want to disturb the neighbors."

Quantril nodded. He took hold of one of the dead man's wrists. With Bauer holding onto the other one, they dragged Meecher's body into the bedroom and propped him up against the dresser.

"I wonder what the rent is on this place," Bauer said.

Quantril laughed. "I don't know. But I think they just had a vacancy."

Bauer grinned before he disappeared through the doorway. With his gun in hand, he checked out the rest of the place. There was no one in the other rooms. From the look of things, the late Al Meecher had lived alone.

When he came back to the living room, Quantril was out on the pocket-sized terrace. "Terrific view," Quantril said, nodding toward the Dream Date building on the opposite side of the street. The tall steel-and-glass structure rose sixty stories upward. On the top, a blinking red light flashed a warning signal to low-flying aircraft.

Leaning against the terrace railing, Bauer peered up at the skyscraper. "This time it's got to work," he said nervously.

"It will. Every detail has been taken care of. All my records will be destroyed, and the annoying matter of those two idiots will be cleared up in the process."

"What if they don't come to the building?"

"Where else would they go?" Quantril said, exasperated. "Your sentries spotted them coming this way, didn't they?"

Bauer nodded.

"And the police weren't with them?"

"No. They must be a couple of thrill seekers or something. No cops within half a mile."

"So it's just a matter of time before they get themselves killed."

"If you say so," Bauer conceded uncertainly.

"I do say so. Do you think I want them alive? I've taken a big loss myself, you know. The whole monastery setup is blown, and I've got all those women to replace." He walked into the living room and slumped down on Meecher's easy chair with a sigh. "It'll work," he said. "They can't get out of this one. The back-up's foolproof."

Bauer was on edge, restless and uneasy. He wandered aimlessly around the living room, picking up the newspaper and then tossing it back to the floor unopened.

"Stop pacing," Quantril ordered. "It's making me nervous."

Bauer forced himself to sit down. "It's just . . ."

"Just what?" Quantril asked irritably.

"I recognized that guy on the roof. Name's Remo Williams. He served under me in Nam."

"So?"

"He's supposed to be dead. I read about it a long time ago. Some drug thing. Williams got the chair."

"Looked like a pretty lively corpse to me."

"It was the same guy. I know it was."

"You're sure you didn't hit him at the monastery?"

"Yeah," Bauer said. "The long-haired kid got in the way."

"Well, you should have," Quantril grumbled. "That mistake's going to come out of your pay."

There was a long silence. Finally Bauer said, "I just don't understand it."

"For God's sake, what now?"

"The way they fought. Williams and that old gook. Christ, he must have been as old as the man in the moon. And Williams is supposed to be *dead*. It just gives me the creeps, that's all."

"Look, he's not a ghost, okay? Take my word for it. Somebody screwed up somewhere. And the other guy might have looked a lot older than he really was. There's nothing supernatural going on. Now will you leave me alone? I have to think."

"Sure, boss," Bauer said. He chewed on his thumbnail to pass five minutes. "You're sure it's going to work?"

"Shut up," Quantril said stonily. "I'll just say it one more time. Those two might be good fighters, but they can't *fly*, got it?"

"Can't—" Bauer smiled. "I guess not."

"Now, we'll just watch for a while until the fun starts. Then we'll be on our way. My office already thinks I'm on vacation in the Alps."

Bauer looked up in surprise. "Is that where we're going?"

Quantril gave him a sly look and shook his head. "No. We're going to a place about three hundred miles south of here called Bayersville."

"A town? You sure it's safe?"

Quantril chuckled. "More than safe. Believe me, you've never seen a town like Bayersville before."

There was a knock at the door. Bauer pulled out his Magnum and walked softly to the wall. Quantril headed for the door. "Who is it?"

"Special delivery." The voice was nasal, with a thick Mexican accent. Quantril nodded to Bauer and opened the door.

Immediately a knife was at his throat. "Throw down your gun, Bauer," Wally Donner said.

"Do it," Quantril rasped.

The Colt clattered to the floor.

Wally Donner edged Quantril into the apartment and slammed the door shut with his foot. "Now, look, I don't want any trouble, Mr. Quantril. I just want my money."

"What money?" Quantril managed, looking wildly toward Bauer.

"The money for keeping quiet about you. Have you seen the papers?"

Bewildered, Bauer picked up the newspaper on the floor and opened it. On the front page was a picture of Karen Lockwood, along with the photos of the now-empty monastery in the Sangre de Cristo Mountains.

"She spilled the beans to the police," Donner said. "Described your little setup to a T. She described you, too, Bauer, and I recognized the description from the times I'd seen you at the rendezvous point when I delivered the women. Only she didn't know your name. I do."

"What's this got to do with me?" Quantril gasped, straining against the blade at his throat.

"I just used my head. All this time I've been wondering about the girls. Who would want two hundred and forty-two women bad enough to lock them up in the hills, I asked myself. And then, after I saw the papers, I asked myself another question. Why *here*, near Santa Fe? And then it came to me. Dream Date. It had to have something to do with Dream Date. So I watched the building until Bauer came out. And guess who was with him?''

Quantril attempted a laugh. ''That's ridiculous. There's no evidence to link me to any of this.''

''Hey, maybe you're forgetting, big shot. I'm not a cop. I don't need evidence. I need money. A million bucks, nothing less—''

Deke Bauer slammed into Donner's head with his elbow, sending him crashing into a wall. Then, before Donner came to enough to pick up the knife, the military man stepped on his right hand. He dug in his heel, feeling the small bones break with satisfying little snaps. While Donner howled in pain, Bauer picked him up by the scruff of the neck and the back of his belt and dragged him to the balcony. Then, with a powerful heave, he tossed Donner over the railing.

There was a sharp wail, followed by a strange bouncing sound. Bauer looked out.

Donner had not fallen on the street below. Instead, he was hanging suspended by one arm and one leg from a flagpole halfway down the building.

''Incredible,'' Quantril said hoarsely behind the soldier.

Bauer rushed back into the room to retrieve his Magnum, but Quantril stopped him.

''I'll just finish him off with one shot,'' Bauer explained.

153

"Don't be a fool. There are already pedestrians on the sidewalk watching."

From the street, they could hear a woman scream, "Look at that!"

"We've got to get out of here," Quantril said. "Now."

"What about him? He'll talk."

"He'll fall first."

"The cops—"

"They'll be busy. Remember?"

CHAPTER FOURTEEN

"I think we take a right here," Remo said as he peered up at the street sign in downtown Santa Fe. "Yeah, this is it." He nodded toward a modern glass building up the block. "And that's the headquarters of Dream Date."

"What a loathesome name for a business enterprise," Chiun said.

"It's Quantril's operation. And if that soldier was right, he does a lot more than play matchmaker."

The building's lobby, as seen from the street, was brightly lit and ultramodern, with a massive steel-and-bronze sculpture as its centerpiece.

"There are no valets here," Chiun complained.

"It's Sunday evening. The building's closed. I figured it was the best time to check Quantril's records." He peered through the window. "Still, there ought to be *someone* here."

He leaned against one of the large glass doors to judge its weight, but to his surprise, they swung open. "I don't get it," Remo said. "There's not a security guard in sight."

Their footfalls echoed through the empty, cavernous lobby. Remo strode silently across the gleaming marble floor to consult the building directory. Dream Date occupied the entire penthouse floor. Across the way he noticed an elevator marked "Penthouse Only."

The unlocked door and the absence of a guard made Remo more than a little suspicious. He couldn't help thinking that their arrival had been anticipated. He wondered what kind of surprises Quantril and his friend, Major Deke Bauer, had in store for them.

"That's the way to the top," Remo said, indicating the private elevator. "Let's go up and take a look around."

Remo pushed the elevator button. The stainless steel doors silently parted. Three men were waiting inside. Each was holding a baseball bat.

"Surprise," one of them said, stepping out. He was so big that he had to stoop to clear the top. Remo slowly took in the bull neck and muscle-corded arms. The man was wearing a garish flowered shirt and lime-green slacks. His bullet-shaped head was bald and shining. His thick, meaty hands were wrapped around a bat. The top hand sported a red ruby ring that winked like a flashing roadmarker.

"Out for a little batting practice, boys?" Remo said in greeting.

"Yeah," the big man answered. "You can be the ball." He whacked the Louisville slugger against his open palm.

The two other men stepped out from the elevator, taking up positions on either side of the bald man. One was black, the other Hispanic.

"What do you guys call yourselves?" Remo asked. "The Bad Breath Bears?"

"Very funny," Flowered Shirt said. "Watch me laugh." He took a mighty swing at Remo's head. The only problem was that by the time the bat reached the place where Remo had been standing, Remo was gone. The bat hit the marble wall with a thunderous crash and splintered into shards.

"How the hell did you do that?" the black man asked.

"Like this." Remo moved one wrist. The next moment, the black man was flying through the air. He screamed as his massive body smashed against the unyielding bronze-and-steel sculpture in the middle of the lobby. His baseball bat went flying.

"Strike one," Remo said.

The Hispanic member of the team took a pace forward. "Willy musta slipped," he said. He raised his bat. "You're gonna pay for that, shithead." The hickory slugger in his hand cut through the air with a sharp, swooshing sound. This time Remo didn't move. A moment before the bat made contact with Remo's neck, he reached out and grabbed its end with two fingers. He pushed, and the bat slid through the Hispanic man's hands like a greased knife, lodging deep in his chest.

"Strike two," Remo said.

The bald, bullet-head man, alone now, blinked a few

times in rapid succession. His forehead creased into a puzzled frown, as he picked up the black man's bat.

"Look out for strike three," Remo said, tapping him on the shoulder. The big man whirled around to find Remo leaning against the elevator doors.

Baldy lunged at him, both hands spread wide on the bat. He slammed it against Remo's throat with all the force in his powerful arms.

Remo exhaled and the bat snapped in two like a discarded toothpick.

The broken bat clattered to the floor as the bald man locked his arms around Remo's neck. "You bastard," he whispered. At close range, the man's breath smelled of meat and cheap wine. His thick fingers edged toward Remo's windpipe. His hooded eyes gleamed as his hands closed on Remo's throat.

"It's language like that that gives the game a bad name," Remo said. He took a half-step, turned his wrist, and the bald man disappeared through the floor of the elevator. Remo heard a high-pitched echoing scream and then a muffled thud from below.

"You're out," Remo called after him.

They walked to the penthouse floor. The foyer was decorated with life-size photos of couples holding hands, skipping along the beach, or staring longingly into one another's eyes. None of the people in the pictures looked as if they would have any trouble finding dates on their own. There was a big teak desk in the unoccupied reception area, and beyond it twin glass doors embellished with

Dream Date's swirling gold logo. Remo padded across the thick cream-colored carpet and tried the doors. Like the ones downstairs, they, too, were unlocked.

"I really don't understand this," Remo said.

"What is so difficult to understand? My reputation has obviously preceded me. The two men you seek, knowing they had an appointment with death, have fled the scene."

Remo shook his head. "I don't know. If there isn't anyone up here, then why did they go to all the bother of providing the welcome wagon in the lobby? Those three clowns weren't just hanging around the elevator for exercise."

Remo was still pondering the situation as he followed Chiun through another pair of double glass doors. They passed under an archway and into a big room lined with desks. On each desk was a small computer terminal and some software. There were some open doors off to the right. Remo poked his head into one of them. There was a video unit, another small computer, a couple of comfortable-looking chairs, and a low table piled with brightly colored brochures.

"This is probably where they bring the clients," Remo said.

Chiun pounded on one of the video units until it shattered to dust. "The man must die," he said.

"Huh? Hey, what are you doing? We're not supposed to wreck the place."

"The person you seek is a sadist. He has filled an entire room with television sets, and none of them has so much as a channel changer."

"There are more doors over there," Remo said, walking past the old man toward yet another area. Through the new set of doors, the atmosphere was radically changed. The sterile, modern furnishings were replaced with high-backed leather chairs, antique tables, and paintings in ornate frames. "I think we're getting close to the boss's office."

They pushed open a door marked "Private." "I'll lay odds this is it," Remo said, surveying the elegant room. Even though there was only a single glass-and-chrome desk inside, the room was bigger than any of the ones they'd been in before. Remo rummaged through the few neatly stacked letters on the desk.

"Nothing," he said. He looked at the shelves of leather-bound books, the wall-sized computer unit, and the giant picture window with its panoramic view of the city.

Remo shrugged. "I don't understand any of this. Not a file, not a phone book. It just doesn't make sense."

Suddenly the computer hummed to life, tiny lights flashing all over the console. Steel panels slid into place, covering the doors, the windows, all possible means of exit from the room. At the same time the carpet began to smolder. Spirals of dancing flame sprang to life in a dozen different locations.

"Now it makes sense," Remo said.

CHAPTER FIFTEEN

A sheet of flame enveloped the carpet with the suddenness of a windswept prairie fire. Noxious blue smoke filled the room, closing around them in swirling clouds.

"Chiun?" Remo called.

"Save the air in your lungs. You will need it."

Remo slowed his breathing. But the smoke still burned and blinded his eyes. He turned around futilely, hoping to spot the steel doors leading to the foyer and the stairs. But the smoke was so thick that he only managed to disorient himself.

"Wait to hear my voice, Little Father. I'm going to break through one of the steel plates into the next room. I think the fire's contained here."

Before Chiun could object, Remo hurled himself feet first toward what he hoped were the doors. He knew as soon as his feet touched a slick surface that shattered under him that he had found the huge picture window instead.

The glass exploded outward with a whoosh of flame. For a moment, Remo was suspended in midair, like all objects before a fall. Through the billowing smoke he caught a glimpse of the street sixty stories below.

Quickly he contracted himself into a tight ball and moved his left shoulder slightly toward the building. The movement gave him just enough impetus to thrust out an arm and catch hold of one of the corners of the blown-out window. The broken glass in the corner cut deep into his hand, but he forced himself to hang on until he could swing his legs back into the room.

It was less smoky now, but the flames were blazing higher. Waves of heat distorted his vision. It was so hot that he could feel his hair singe. A small bony hand touched his and deposited a ball of silk cloth into it to stem the bleeding.

"We go up," Chiun said. Raising his arm, the old man crouched and turned slightly. There was almost no breath coming from him, so complete was his concentration. Then he spiraled upward, crashing through the ceiling in a burst of pure power. After the rain of debris from his exit settled, Remo spun on his right foot and glided up to follow Chiun through the narrow opening.

The two men stood on a gravel rooftop. It felt good to breathe again. Above them was the night sky, silent and dotted with stars. Too silent.

"Do you know what's funny?" Remo asked.

"This is not an appropriate time for humor."

"What's funny is that no fire alarm went off. Quantril must want to burn his own building down."

"Take another time to ponder the eccentricities of strangers," Chiun said. "Let us climb down from this uncomfortable place." He threw his legs over the side, but a column of flame shot up beside him, and he retracted quickly back to the center of the roof. More flames from below surged up, encircling the top of the building as the wind whipped the fire up to astonishing heights.

"There is only one solution," Chiun said grimly.

"The Flying Wall?"

"Never. There are automobiles on the street. We would be killed. What is required is four separate movements. First, a simple arching dive."

"Toward what?"

"The building across the street."

"I can't even see it," Remo said.

"It is there. Next, a half-turn. This is done quickly, to halt your speed. Then you move slowly into the Falcon's Glide. Remember when I made you practice cliff-diving? That is it. The last part is delicate. You must flatten yourself against the building on the inhaled breath."

"What happens if I'm exhaling?"

Chiun clucked. "Do not find out," he said, shaking his head. "Follow me." The old man stretched out his arms and leaped off the side, into the flames.

Remo followed. He could feel the heat against his face and chest. His eyes were closed, and the inside of his eyelids were colored a bright orange.

At the peak of the dive, when he felt he was losing

163

speed, Remo did a fast half-turn, halting himself in the middle of empty space. Then he drew a breath and soared downward in a perfect Falcon's Glide, his back rigid, his head raised.

He relaxed his body as he felt the space in front of him being filled with the form of another building. Chiun was right. It had been there. He sucked in his breath on impact. He could feel his body shake like a willow in the wind. His cut hand sent a shriek of pain through him as it slapped against the sandstone wall, but his grasp held.

He felt around with his feet, and found the top of a window ledge. It was an old-fashioned apartment building, with real sills. It would be an easy climb down. Remo felt his breath come easier.

He had not failed again.

Below, a crowd of onlookers gathered on the street. Fire engines began to wail in the distance. Chiun's white tousled head bobbed at the level of the sixth or seventh floor. But there was something else between him and Chiun, something that made him shake his head as he descended and wonder if he were seeing things.

At the twelfth story, there appeared to be a man hanging from a flagpole. As he neared, he could hear the man's hoarse screams. "Help me," he called wildly to Remo. He tried to wave, as if the man climbing inexplicably down the side of the building could miss seeing him.

"Hold still," Remo said. "I'll get you."

"They tried to kill me," the man babbled. "I don't know what they wanted the girls for. All I wanted was some money."

"Tell me later. Now, when I come close, just grab hold of my shoulder with your free hand."

"I can't," the man wailed. "My hand's broken."

"That's great," Remo mumbled. "Well, just sit tight. I'll get you."

He descended carefully, veering toward the man on the flagpole. The blood from his hand left a long red streak behind him. When at last he reached the man, he felt tentatively with his arm, and located a spot on the middle of the man's back. Then, in a smooth, strong motion, Remo pulled the man off the pole and flung him behind himself so that the man landed on Remo's back.

The man was screaming for all he was worth.

"Relax, will you?" Remo said. "We're almost there."

"Wha . . . wha . . ." Slowly, the man opened his squeezed-shut eyes. "I didn't fall," he marveled. Then he gasped as he realized he had somehow landed on Remo's back. "How did . . . It was so fast."

"I don't give out trade secrets, so don't ask," Remo said.

He deposited the man on the ground. The crowd burst into spontaneous applause. Chiun bowed to them, smiling serenely. A van with the call letters of a TV station was hurtling down the street toward them.

"Let's go, Little Father," Remo prompted.

"Hey, wait a minute." It was the man Remo had rescued, his legs wobbling like lengths of rubber hose. "I've got to talk to you."

"Save your thanks," Remo said.

"It's not about thanks. It's about Quantril and Bauer.

165

I think you were the guys they were trying to get rid of."

"Quantril and Bauer? Do you know where they went?"

The man's face transformed suddenly. Instead of the frightened, disheveled person who was certain he was going to die a horrible death, there now stood before Remo a smirking, oily-looking creature ready to deal. "Maybe," he said slyly.

"What do you mean, maybe?" Remo yelled so loud his voice cracked.

"Let's talk," the man said, smiling now.

His legs were not wobbling any longer.

Wally Donner led them through a series of winding alleyways to an inconspicuous-looking building. Inside, he opened the door to a small but impeccably furnished apartment.

"Sit down," he said, flashing a smile.

"No thanks. What do you want?"

"I think I'd like a yacht," Donner said dreamily. "A place on the Riviera. A bathroom made of black marble. Maybe a little pied-à-terre in Paris."

"What do you think this is, a quiz show?"

"Do you want to know where Bauer and Quantril are?" he teased.

Remo looked him up and down. "How would you know that anyway?"

Donner lit a cigarette. "They were in the building you came down. Killed the guy who lived in the apartment just so they could watch you two burn up. I heard them planning it. I was outside the apartment door. That's how I know where they're going. And I'll tell you—for a price.''

"I just saved your life!" Remo exploded.

"Yes. And don't think I don't appreciate it. But a guy's got to make a living, you know?" He shrugged expressively.

"Break his elbows," Chiun suggested.

"Then I'll never talk. And they'll come after you again."

Remo sighed. The ingrate would talk, all right. But Remo was hot and dirty, and not at all in the mood to break anybody's elbows, even if it was for a good cause. He reached into his pocket and pulled out a roll of bills. "All right. How much do you want?"

"A million dollars," Donner said.

"Here's eight hundred. Take it or leave it."

Donner hesitated only a moment before snatching the money.

"Perhaps you can build a bathroom of concrete blocks with that," Chiun said.

"There's another thing," Donner said as he counted the money. "A promise. You seem like a man who's good to his word."

"I am," Remo said.

"Then I want your word that you won't kill me."

"You mean to get back the money? You got it."

"You promise?"

"We both do," Remo said magnanimously.

Donner stepped back carefully, edging toward the door. "Okay. They're headed for a place called Bayersville, about three hundred miles south of here. It's a ghost town."

"Have you been there?"

"I read about it once in a movie magazine. They used to shoot a lot of low-budget Westerns there back in the fifties. Quantril owns the town now. He uses it for his Dream Date videos."

Donner opened the door to leave.

"Wait a second," Remo called. "Just to satisfy my curiosity . . . How do you know Quantril?"

Donner smiled. "I think I used to work for him," he said. "Running illegals across the Mexican border."

Remo felt the blood rush out of his face. "Women?"

"The ones I kept were women, yes." He flashed another dazzling smile, then went out, closing the door behind him.

Remo clenched his teeth. He had just found the man who'd murdered 300 people in the desert. And let him go.

CHAPTER SIXTEEN

The lights of the rented car passed over a weathered road sign. "Bayersville," it announced in peeling, sun-faded letters. "Just Watch Us Grow." In spite of the optimistic prediction, the only growth that Remo could see were the weeds and wild flowers that overran the rutted dirt road.

As they passed over a bumpy rise, the town came into view, shimmering in the moonlight. There were four blocks of buildings, including a church, a bank, a saloon, a few shops. From a distance, Bayersville looked exactly like a fictional town of the Old West. It was only up close that one noticed that the buildings were really false-fronted, weather-beaten structures with no breath of life in them.

As Remo drove past the sagging buildings, the sight of them stirred something in his memory. Suddenly he knew. It was the movies at St. Theresa's.

In the orphanage where Remo grew up, the biggest

treats the nuns had to offer were the once-a-month movies. All of the kids would gather in the basement, impatient and restless while Sister Mary Agnes threaded the ancient projector.

The movies they saw were donated by a local theater owner, so they were rarely Hollywood's newest or best. They also had to pass Sister Bridget's rigid code of inspection that made the Hays Office look like a hotbed of libertines and panderers. So mostly they saw Westerns, the old-fashioned kind with Straight Shooters in white hats and Bad Hombres in black ones. The films never had much in the way of plot. It was good against evil, pure and simple. And in the end, although things looked kind of close for a while, good always carried the day. For a time, when he was very young, Remo had believed that that was the way the world actually was, all black and white, with nothing in between.

Vietnam and the Newark police department had put that idea to rest forever. Still, Remo felt a childish delight as he drove through the silent town. There was the saloon where Red Ryder had shot it out with the counterfeiters and, across the way, the stable where John Wayne had leaped into the saddle from the hayloft above. Bayersville was a ghost town, silent as death, populated only by the shadows of yesterday's heroes.

And two other men who were real. And dangerous.

Remo parked the car in front of the boarded-up Empire Hotel. "We might as well start here," he said.

The moment their feet touched the dusty street, they were engulfed in a powerful, glaring light. There was no explosion, just a fizzing sound, like soda being poured from a bottle, to break the silence. The town and everything else seemed to disappear in the pure white light.

Then, as quickly as it had come, the light vanished. In its place was total darkness.

"Welcome to Bayersville," a voice called out from the rooftop above. Remo recognized it as Deke Bauer's. "I didn't think you'd be out here, but when I saw the car coming, I figured you two might be coming for a short visit. Real short." He laughed.

You surprised me once, Remo said to himself. *It's not going to happen again.* "Just keep talking, Bauer."

The major's harsh laughter grew louder. "Honest, I'm glad you came. Now I can finish what I started. That is, unless you brought someone along to throw himself in front of you when the shooting starts. That's your style, isn't it, Williams?"

"Don't—" Chiun began, but Remo's anger was stronger than his reason. He leaped blindly toward the voice. But just as he left the ground, his balance was thrown by a thundering blast of music. It was marching music turned up to an unbearably high level, its brass and drums blaring like the shock waves of an explosion.

Remo slammed into the roof, out of control, and toppled over backward, hitting the bumpy road below. The loud music masked all other sounds. He couldn't see Bauer in the sudden darkness, and now he couldn't hear him, either. He strained to pick out the sound of footsteps, but it was impossible. Everything was drowned out by the crash of cymbals and the high, piercing notes of a dozen or more cornets.

Remo made himself relax, and in a few moments his eyes adjusted to the darkness. But all he could see around him were the car and the deserted buildings. Chiun was gone.

He started to look for the old man, but a sharp jolt of pain stabbed into his shoulder. A fraction of a second later, he heard the crack of the bullet.

"Bauer," he hissed. All of the hate he had felt for the man welled up inside him again.

Don't, he told himself. *Don't let him get to you again.* The past is gone, as dead as the ghosts in this place. Remember who you are *now*. Now is what matters. Nothing else.

He felt the sticky flow of blood as it seeped through his fingers. Another shot ricocheted off the car with a metallic whine. As best as Remo could judge, it had landed a few inches right of his head. He rolled, trying frantically to find Bauer's form on one of the darkened rooftops.

It occurred to him then that he might well die in this place. What a stupid way to go, he thought—listening to an army marching song. He winced as air began to work its way into the wound. Why didn't Bauer just finish him off? The arrogant bastard was playing with Remo, gloating over his handiwork. But, then, Remo should have expected that Bauer would play this out for all it was worth. He remembered the bodies on the wire.

"Forget it," Remo said out loud, as if the words would calm his fears. "Now. Only now."

Lurching to his feet, he skittered down the street, keeping close to the buildings. If Bauer was going to kill him, he'd have to work for it.

Suddenly the music stopped. Remo shook his head to clear the ringing in his ears. In the distance he could hear a board creak under the pressure of a heavy foot.

Remo flattened himself against the side of a building. It was marked "General Store," and Bauer was inside. The footsteps moved in one direction and then another, exploring. At last they headed toward the street.

And Remo was ready. *Now. Only now.*

At the first quiver of the swinging doors, Remo burst through, kicking Bauer's weapon clear.

Bauer hit without hesitation. He dug his fist directly into Remo's shoulder wound. Remo screamed and reeled backward. Bauer came after him, delivering a powerful kick between Remo's legs. As Remo doubled over in pain, Bauer picked the Colt off the ground and sauntered calmly over to where Remo lay.

"You know what I'm going to do?" he asked softly. His lips were curved in a malicious smile. "First, I'm going to shoot you—not kill you, Williams, just air-condition you a little." His eyes shone. "And then I'm going to put up a wire." He stretched the word out until it seemed to pull with it a thousand nightmare memories. "Remember the wire, Williams?" He stepped back a pace and cocked the safety.

Now . . . only now . . . nothing else. . . .

"I remember," Remo said, too quietly to hear. And the gun fired, but Remo was not there, and the next moment

173

Bauer's face twisted in surprise as a foot came out of nowhere and sent him crashing against a post that splintered and broke under his weight.

Then Remo was on him, dragging him back into the street, shoving him to the ground, his fingers wound around Bauer's thick, corded neck.

"Don't," Bauer gurgled. "It isn't—"

"Where's Quantril?"

Spittle oozed out of the corners of Bauer's mouth. "The saloon." His bulging eyes looked at Remo expectantly, but the pressure around his neck did not lessen. "Be fair," he pleaded. "Remember . . ."

"I do," Remo said softly. "That's the trouble." His fingertips met.

"Chiun?" Remo whispered. There was no answer.

Leaving Bauer's body on the street, he walked the block to the Bayersville saloon. As he neared it, he heard tinkling music from the player piano and the sound of voices.

The saloon was lit with colored gaslights. Remo stopped short in the doorway for a moment, because the place seemed to be filled with people. Voluptuous girls, their hair piled on their heads, their long dresses lifted to the ankle to reveal high-button shoes, danced with bearded, burly men in antique suits. But he saw quickly that the people were only images projected on the saloon's walls. The place was empty except for one man seated alone at a table near the stairway in the back.

"Quantril?" Remo said, approaching him.

The man nodded elegantly. "I really never thought

you'd get this far," he said. "You're quite a remarkable man."

"Where's Chiun?"

"Who? Oh, your Oriental friend. He's fine."

"I didn't ask how he is. I want to know where."

Quantril ignored him. He spread his arms in a gesture encompassing the room. "How do you like my town, Mr. Williams?"

"I can think of places I'd rather be."

"The saloon is one of Dream Date's most popular fantasy settings."

"Dream Date's history, Quantril."

"Nonsense."

"There's a matter of a couple of hundred women you kept as prisoners against their will."

Quantril shook his head like an indulgent father addressing a child. "That can't be linked to me. It was Deke Bauer's operation. He's dead, I presume."

"That's right."

"Excellent. You spared me the bother."

"You booby-trapped your own building."

"That's what you say. But from the evidence, it looks like you and your ancient friend broke in, killed three security guards, and then set the penthouse on fire, destroying all my records. They were in the computer." He burst into laughter. "If the police want anyone, it'll be you."

Remo exhaled noisily. Quantril was exactly the kind of criminal CURE had been devised to stop. The law couldn't touch him. Remo could. But not until he had found Chiun.

"What about the guy who led us here? You left him for dead. Do you think he won't talk?"

"Wally Donner? Don't make me laugh. He's got a criminal record a mile long. A psychopathic killer. The minute he shows his face, he'll be escorted to a psychiatric ward."

"Wally Donner, is it?" Remo brightened. At least he had a name now. But he'd have to try a bluff.

He shrugged. "Well, it looks like you've got the rap beaten, Quantril. Nobody'll arrest you."

"Thank you."

"Because I'm going to kill you first."

"Not so fast," Quantril said, smiling. "There's one small matter. You see, through the years I've made a sort of hobby of explosives. Keeps my fingers busy. This is one of the places I practiced on."

Remo felt his skin tightening.

"In fact, I've rigged the entire town of Bayersville to blow up like a rocket in . . ." He checked his watch. "Sixty seconds."

"I don't think so," Remo said. "You don't look like the suicidal type."

"Oh, I'm not planning to die. It would ruin my plans for the future. You only interrupted them. You haven't really changed a thing."

Remo could hear his internal clock ticking away the seconds. "Where's Chiun?" he demanded.

"I'll give him to you. All I ask of you in return is a head start."

"What about this so-called bomb?"

"I'll deactivate it as soon as you say yes."

Remo thought about it. "You're lying," he said.

"Eleven seconds, Mr. Williams. Ten. Nine. Eight . . ."

He couldn't take the chance. "All right."

"A wise decision," Quantril said. He took a key from his pocket, inserted it in a small box in the wall by the stairway, and turned it. The projected images faded from the walls. The tinkling music stopped. Quantril climbed the stairs.

"How about your part of the deal?" Remo called.

"Behold," Quantril said from the darkness of the stairway. A panel in the far wall slid open to reveal the old Oriental, gagged and tied to a chair.

"Chiun!"

Above, a helicopter whirred to life.

The Korean burst out of his bonds in a frenzy. "Fool! You let him go!"

"He was going to blow the place up, and you with it," Remo explained.

Chiun shot him a black look. "You are even more ignorant than I thought," he said as he raced toward the stairs. "Do you think a piece of twine can hold the Master of Sinanju?"

"It sure looked that way," Remo said, following.

"Idiot. I only let that perfumed fop tie me up so that he would stop that infernal music. We must hurry. Faster, Remo."

"There's no way we can catch that chopper, Chiun. We'll just have to track Quantril down—"

"Where? In Paradise?"

"What are you talking about?"

Chiun sighed. "Like all criminals, he felt the need to boast. So while I permitted him to tie me up, I listened to his prattle. I wanted to know if there were others. The bomb was not activated when you came in."

The stairs led upward to a trapdoor. Remo left it open as he climbed onto the roof. "So he's a liar," he said. Quantril's helicopter was beginning to lift off.

"Yes. It was activated when he turned off the movie pictures."

"The . . . oh, God."

Remo lunged for the helicopter, hooking his arm around the rudders. "Jump!" he yelled as the machine lifted him into the air. "Chiun, jump!"

Somersaulting upward, Remo kicked open the helicopter door. Miles Quantril's elegance deserted him as Remo pulled him out of the pilot's seat and dangled him from the open door.

"You can't do this!" he screamed. "I'm Miles Quantril! This is barbaric!"

"That's the biz, sweetheart," Remo said as he dropped him.

Quantril made a perfect one-point dive into the open trapdoor on the roof of the saloon. Remo jumped a moment later, twisting as he fell so that he landed in the weeds next to Chiun behind Bayersville's one street.

The helicopter, now abandoned, careened downward, its engine stalled. It hit the ground with a boom, then exploded into flame.

"If there really is a bomb, it'll go now," Remo said. "We'd better get as far away as we can."

The two of them dashed at top speed toward the distant hills. They just made it past the weather-beaten sign announcing Bayersville when the explosion came.

The very earth seemed to crack open with an earsplitting roar as every building in the deserted village blew apart in a Technicolor spectacle of destruction.

Something inside Remo hurt more than the wound in his shoulder while he watched the old familiar movie setting collapse and disappear in a sea of flame.

It never really existed, he told himself. Red Ryder and John Wayne had only been in movies, and their adventures were no more than a harmless way for an orphanage full of lonely kids to pass the time. But part of Remo still remembered the heroes who once rode down the town's single dusty street on their magnificent steeds to set things right and make the world fine again, and that part of him ached.

"Let's go," he mumbled, feeling old. There was nothing more to be seen in Bayersville. When the fires settled, he knew, nothing would remain of it except a few charred bits of stone and wood, along with the fading, splendid ghosts from its past.

CHAPTER SEVENTEEN

Wally Donner staggered out of the bar, leaned against a parked car, and threw up in the gutter. His head was reeling and his stomach churned from the two dozen Scotches he'd consumed in the sleazy Mexico City bar where he'd spent the past five hours. There was a bitter aftertaste in his throat, and his temples throbbed rhythmically, as if a tiny mariachi band were playing inside his head.

The horrible part of it was that the band was playing Mexican music. It was bad enough to have to listen to strumming guitars and maracas in every corner of this godforsaken place, but now even his own mind was betraying him.

Donner gritted his teeth and wiped the crust of vomit from his mouth with the back of his hand. He hated Mexican music. He hated Mexican food. He hated sombreros and sandals made out of used tires. But most of all, he hated Mexico, which was where he was going to have to live for the next few years if he wanted to avoid a long stretch in a state penitentiary.

"Get back to the hotel room," he commanded himself. But it was so damn hard to think with that band playing in his head. He drew a deep breath and staggered out into the street. He could see his shiny new van parked on the other side of it.

Donner was almost there when the old Ford turned the corner and sent him flying into traffic. In the split second before death took him, he saw the tiny Virgin Mary on the dashboard flanked by two tiny flags.

"Mexico," he screamed.

Suddenly the dance band stopped playing.

Remo, Chiun, and Harold W. Smith sat at a candlelit table in one of Santa Fe's best restaurants.

"We're here under the name of Hossenfecker," Smith said with his usual paranoia.

"Ah. Very good, Emperor. It is so much less conspicuous than 'Smith.' "

Smith rustled the papers in front of him. "It was my mother's name," he mumbled. "At any rate, I have the information you asked for." He cleared his throat. "Wally, a.k.a. José Donner. Recently deceased in Mexico City."

"What?" Remo asked, incredulous.

"Automobile accident. He had in his possession a Ruger Blackhawk that matches the bullets found in the bodies scattered over the mesa. Er, good work, both of you."

"A car accid—"

"It was nothing," Chiun said hastily, kicking Remo under the table. "When fortune comes your way, accept it," he added in Korean.

"I beg your pardon?" Smith asked.

"A little indigestion, Emperor," Chiun said sweetly.

"Oh. Well, the second person you wanted to know about, this Samuel P. Wolfshy . . ."

"Go on," Remo said.

Smith made a face. "I'm not sure he's the right man. The information on him was very scanty. According to my records, this person has never worked."

"That's him."

Chiun leaned forward eagerly. "Yes. Do tell what has become of our young brave."

This time Remo kicked Chiun. "Not that we know him, Smitty. He never saw us. After all, we don't leave witnesses."

"I should hope not," Smith said. "Well, it seems Mr. Wolfshy encountered some good fortune."

"Hey, great," Remo said.

Smith slapped down his papers. "He *was* just a bystander, wasn't he? The statement he gave to the police said that he arrived at the monastery after everything had already been settled, and that he was shot accidentally while picking up an abandoned firearm."

"Right," Remo said. "Absolutely."

Smith shot him a suspicious look. "Then why are you so interested in him?"

"I saw his picture in the paper," Remo said glibly. "He looked like he might be a distant cousin of mine."

Smith's eyes narrowed, but he let it pass. "Very well," he said. "After this Wolfshy recovered from his wound, he married a woman named Consuela Madera in Las Vegas. Two days after the wedding, he apparently borrowed a quarter from the doorman of a downtown casino, put it in a slot machine, and won approximately one point nine million dollars."

Remo's face went blank. "What?"

"Right now he's making inquiries about starting a bank on an Indian reservation. The Kanton Savings and Loan."

He folded his papers, then carefully burned them in the ashtray. "Anything else?"

"I'll be damned," Remo said.

Chiun gasped, jerking his chair backward and clutching at his heart.

Remo jumped up. "Chiun! Are you—"

"It is she!" He pointed a trembling finger toward the entrance, where a matronly looking blond woman wearing a fur coat entered. "Mona Madrigal!" He pulled himself to his feet. "Thank you, most kind and gracious Emperor," he said formally.

Smith stared at the old man above his steel-rimmed spectacles. "Er . . . think nothing of it," he said.

When Chiun had wafted away toward the husky woman, Smith turned to Remo. "Who is this Mona Madrigal?"

"A woman Chiun thinks you gave him."

Chiun was ecstatic as he bowed to the actress. The fates had decreed their meeting, and thus did it happen. "It is I," he announced in a cheerful singsong.

"Step aside, shorty," Mona answered in a deep whiskey voice.

Chiun looked around him. Whoever "shorty" was, he had apparently beat a hasty retreat. "Chiun, Master of Sinanju, offers you the tribute of his adoration."

"No kiddin'." She waved over his head. "Hey, Walt! Walt!"

The maitre d' came rushing over. "Yes, madame?"

She cocked her head toward Chiun. "Do me a favor, hon, and give this bum the rush."

The tuxedoed gentleman glared at Chiun. "Sir, perhaps you're wanted at your table."

"Oh, it's quite all right. They'll wait," Chiun said affably. "Miss Madrigal, I gaze at your countenance each day on 'As the Planet Revolves.' "

She burst into strident laughter. "What? That piece of shit? They wouldn't let me show so much as one tit on that show. It almost wrecked my career."

Chiun stepped back, his mouth gaping. "I . . . I . . ."

"Amscray, Pops," she said, elbowing her way past him.

The old Oriental stood where he was for a long moment, his white hair drooping like a melting ice cream cone. Then, taking a deep breath, he came quietly back to the table.

Remo hurt for him. "I'm sorry, Little Father," he said.

Chiun shrugged. "It was a disappointment, but the world can be a thoughtless place."

"That's the spirit," Remo said, patting him on the back.

"However, I must write to Miss Madrigal immediately."

"After that? What for?"

"To tell her that there is in her very city a vile, coarse woman attempting to impersonate her, of course."

"What?"

Chiun bent low over the table and whispered, "Obviously that woman is in the service of some foreign power determined to shatter my serenity and sour my disposition."

Remo stared at him for a moment, blinking. "Obviously," he said at last.

"It may be a conspiracy. Perhaps you would like to look into the matter yourself, Emperor."

Harold Smith choked on his water. "Er . . . yes. That is, I'll see what I can do."

The old man grinned with satisfaction as he picked up his cup of tea and sipped it. "It is a good feeling," he said, "to associate with reasonable men."

The Destroyer
Warren Murphy

CELEBRATING 10 YEARS IN PRINT
AND OVER 22 MILLION COPIES SOLD!